Hope
Springs

❋

ALSO BY LYNNE HINTON

Friendship Cake
The Things I Know Best
Forever Friends
Meditations for Walking

Hope Springs

A NOVEL

❋

Lynne Hinton

Originally published under the title *Garden of Faith*

HarperSanFrancisco
A Division of HarperCollins*Publishers*

HarperOne

HarperCollins books may be purchased for educational, business, or sales promotional use. For information please write: Special Markets Department, HarperCollins Publishers, 10 East 53rd Street, New York, NY 10022.

HarperCollins Web site: http://www.harpercollins.com
HarperCollins®, ■®, and HarperOne™ are trademarks of
HarperCollins Publishers.

FIRST HARPERCOLLINS PAPERBACK EDITION PUBLISHED IN 2003
Designed by Joseph Rutt
Excerpt from *Forever Friends* copyright © by Lynne Hinton

Library of Congress Cataloging-in-Publication Data
Hinton, J. Lynne.
Hope springs : a novel / Lynne Hinton. — 1st ed.
p. cm.
ISBN 978-0-06-251747-0
1. Women gardeners—Fiction. 2. Female friendship—Fiction.
3. Gardening—Societies, etc.—Fiction. I. Title.
PS3558.I457 G37   2002
813'.54—dc21   2001051540

10 11 12 13 14 RRD(H) 10 9 8 7 6

Dedicated to the memory of
Lessie Alford
and
in honor of
Jack and Shirley Hinton
and
with much gratitude to
my friends at
HarperSanFrancisco

IN YOUR GARDEN NOW

Grass grows now tall and tangled
where your cucumbers and melons
once rolled in tight bunches
green and gathered.

You'd clench your fists and draw in your lips
with worry if you caught sight of what roams
in your garden now.

Shaking your head in horror, you'd be up before the sun
raking and ridding the ground
of clover and prickly vines,
pigweed, and dandelions.

You'd mmmm, mm, mmm the rows
until those weeds bowed in shame
and pushed themselves up
making room for your
beans and sunripe tomatoes.

You'd dance upon the earth until she gave you back
your delicate pansies and long, limber sunflowers.

And she'd forget that you left her.

And you'd smooth down the dirt
with sprinkles of water that lay like teardrops
in the prints you made neatly
between the plants.

And together you and the earth
would spring forth flowers and fruit
rich and bountiful.

And together you and the earth
would celebrate harvest and tolerate winter
until the air warmed and the low blanket rose.

And you would smile and say
I'll go to my garden now.

But now the earth has you buried
deep within her bosom
way beneath what tickles her surface
and spreads across her skin
in meadows and fields.

And she cannot stop the clover and the prickly vines
from thickening
nor can she stop
the pigweed and the dandelions
that fill up her furrowed brow.

So she reaches inside herself
just to feel you there and covers your eyes
so as not to worry you
with what lies
in your garden now.

Hope Springs Community Garden Club Newsletters

Contents

Hope Springs Community Garden Club Newsletter

BEA'S BOTANICAL BITS

Looking at Your Landscape

Beginning a garden is a little like starting a relationship. You got to know before you hoe. And, ladies, you know what I'm talking about. There are things you must find out about your partner before you decide to invest a lot of time and work in the friendship. It's the same for your gardening. You don't just decide that you like a place and start cultivating it without discovering things about the area. You need to examine the proposed spot for property borders, service-line locations, septic tanks, and leach fields. The condition of the soil, the amount of sunlight, the plants native to that area, these all need to be noted before breaking ground and sowing seed.

You want your relationship to work and evolve into the lovely state of matrimony? Then don't let yourself be surprised by what you didn't take the time to find out early in the relationship. You want a productive garden? Learn the landscape before you do the work.

I

$\mathcal{S}$AFETY IS OF THE LORD'S was printed in three-foot-tall red letters, stretched high and wide across the back of the transfer truck that pulled out in front of Charlotte as she drove Highway 85 heading toward Chapel Hill.

"Jesus!" was all she said as she slammed on brakes and swerved onto the shoulder to avoid hitting it. And then, "Shit." It wasn't until after the word had spilled out of her mouth, loud and unmistakably clear, that she remembered a church member was sitting next to her. She turned to her right to see if Beatrice was okay.

The older woman was pale but certainly fine, having reached out in front of her, bracing herself for the collision. White-knuckled and rigid, she softened as the car rolled forward and finally stopped. Since the near miss was over, she blew out a noisy puff of air. Seconds later she loosened her grip and released her hands from the curved black plastic, touched at the hair on her forehead, and asked, "My God, is that from the Old or the New Testament?"

There were prints from her fingers still showing on the dashboard.

Charlotte had pulled off to the side of the road and put the car into park. She closed her eyes and dropped her chin to her chest. Her heart was pounding. She hadn't had such a close call on the highway in a long time. It unnerved her and she knew that she needed a few minutes to get herself together. Other vehicles flew past them, almost lifting the little car back onto the road. Finally, Charlotte turned to Beatrice, remembering that she had asked a question.

"Is what from the Old or New Testament?" She was still rattled.

"That sentence." Beatrice smoothed out the front of her dress and tugged at her panty hose.

Charlotte was confused. She shrugged her shoulders as if to signal that she wasn't following Beatrice's line of thinking.

"On that truck. It said 'Safety is of the Lord's.' Is that from before or after Jesus?"

Charlotte then remembered the sign on the truck. She shook her head at the question while putting the car into gear. She signaled and pulled onto the interstate slowly. "It's from a psalm, I guess." She looked in her rearview mirror and watched as the cars behind them moved into the left lanes, allowing her space to merge.

"It's nice, I think." Beatrice lowered the visor and began studying herself in the mirror.

Charlotte started to mention the irony of such a quotation on a vehicle that had almost crushed them; but as she turned to say something to Beatrice, the older woman already seemed to have forgotten what she'd said. She was reaching down on the floorboard to open her purse. She took out her lipstick and painted her lips bright pink, as if the near wreck had reminded her to do what she usually never forgot, "be ready." She flipped up the visor, smacking her lips together, and offered the lipstick to Charlotte, who raised her hand and politely refused.

"No, of course not, pink is not your color." Beatrice put the cover on the lipstick and stowed it in her purse. She took a breath.

"Have you seen the Mary Kay samples for fall? There's some

lovely corals and mauves that I think would match your fair skin and dark hair nicely. And I believe we can find some eye pencils that will draw out that gold in your eyes."

Charlotte did not reply.

For some time now, Beatrice had been trying to help her pastor "find her colors" and "perk up her wardrobe." She seemed satisfied that Charlotte no longer needed a hobby or craft to occupy her time, but she continued to struggle with the idea that the young woman acted as if she did not care about her appearance.

Louise told Charlotte that Beatrice had found an article in some magazine she picked up on her honeymoon that said that failure to show interest in basic grooming skills was a sign of depression. Louise had told her that if that were the case, then depression might come in handy for Charlotte, who she knew was trying to save money, since blush and eye shadow could be quite expensive; and that Louise, in her entire life, had never worn makeup and she did not consider herself depressed. But Beatrice wasn't worried about Louise. She was worried about Charlotte.

In the last few months, the young preacher seemed to have folded within herself in a way that was subtle but still noticeable. She continued to do her work, preach, visit, all the things that were expected; but there was a distance in her conversations, a lack of focus that even Margaret had observed. She, of course, had said to let it alone, that Charlotte would discover her own way through this, but Beatrice was convinced that she could find something in her cosmetic bag that might help, even if just a little.

Charlotte picked up speed. The late morning sun poured into the car and she began to get warm, so she increased the volume of the air conditioner and turned the vents toward her, hoping the noise might also limit any further conversation.

Unlike Beatrice, she did not think of herself as depressed. She did not think she had changed. She knew that she felt more tired than usual, a little uninterested in things at hand. But she only thought she was overworked, called her lack of energy and her sleeplessness the result of too many appointments and a crazy schedule that recently had included late-night emergency calls to the hospital, three summer weddings, and now this, another suicide attempt by Nadine Klenner.

Since the accident and Brittany's death, Nadine had become broken and unhinged in a way that seemed completely hopeless. Nothing nor anyone was able to help. Her spiral down into despair started with the use of Valium and other prescribed drugs, just to get through the night, she had told the doctor. Then she went to cheaper means of escape, alcohol, over-the-counter medications, and even a little pot she was able to get from some guy who had moved in down the street from where she lived.

Her first attempt, at Christmas, had been a bad mix of wine and drugs; but she claimed she had just made a mistake in taking too many sleeping pills. After she promised to get into counseling, the doctor released her without a follow-up.

The second time, a Monday morning in April, Nadine got up in the middle of the night. She called Charlotte, just to talk, she had said; but Charlotte knew something was wrong. By the time the preacher was able to call 911 and get over to the house, Nadine had passed out in the bathtub, the cuts on the insides of her wrists deep but fresh; and they were able to stop the bleeding before that attempt had become successful. She went to a rehab for three months.

This time she was visiting a friend, her mother said. They had gone out for dinner; it was Brittany's birthday. The friend told the police that things had been fine, that Nadine had been sad and wanted to get back home early to put flowers on the grave, but that she seemed okay. And then, just as they were leaving the restaurant, she said something like "Maybe the best way is the same way" and stepped off the curb right into oncoming traffic. She was hit by a taxi and thrown across the street.

She was in a regular room at the University Hospital since the medical doctor did not know that this was Nadine's idea of a fair and easy way to die. He merely thought she had been distracted or nonattentive when she had tried to cross a busy street.

Hopefully, Charlotte thought, somebody has realized that this was no accident and when Nadine is stronger, they'll move her to the psychiatric unit. Of course she knew that didn't mean it could be fixed. Charlotte understood that if a person is set on dying, no pill or therapy or suicide watch on a hospital floor where all the doors are locked can stop it. If Nadine meant to kill herself, Charlotte didn't really think there was anything that could be done to prevent it.

"I hope these balloon flowers aren't too much for Nadine's room. I wanted to bring some of my lavender border phlox but they had the spider mites, so I just picked a few of these." Beatrice had the vase of flowers in a box near her feet. Luckily they had not turned over in the sudden stop.

Beatrice kept talking about the pests in her garden, but Charlotte heard none of it. She was thinking about her recent

decision to plant geraniums and late marigolds around the front
door of the parsonage. She had gone to a store and bought some
flowers, even though the clerk said it was too late for them to grow
and that she would not be able to get a refund if they died and that
maybe she should wait for the pansies.

She recalled finding roots and vines around the porch and discovering that there was too much shade from the big sweet gum
near the driveway so that she had to change the location of her little
flower bed. She remembered walking around searching for a place
to plant the flowers and noticing a spot near the clothesline that
seemed to have sandy soil and could have been a site once before
for someone's garden, although now it was primarily ignored and
weedy. She thought of how, after she bought the plants and the
wrong fertilizer, she had roamed about the yard seeing the places
where things used to grow and areas that could never support vegetables and flowers, rocky patches and deep rich soil, sites she'd
never noticed until she really paid attention.

As Beatrice babbled on about daylilies, potato bugs, and her
monthly articles in the Hope Springs Garden Club newsletter,
Charlotte reflected upon the landscape of somebody's life. She
thought about Nadine and her struggle to stay alive. She thought
about Louise and Roxie and the things people never tell. She thought
about how complicated one person can be, a single life in a world of
lives hidden with plots and stretches that will not nurture a seed, beds
that cover poison and electric lines and should never be cultivated.
Slopes that drain and collect water. Spots that never see the sun. And
the young minister wondered how people can ever really heal and
grow if they do not recognize and honor their limitations, deal with
the secrets and the trouble areas, walk the land on which they live.

She thought about her own heart and the condition of her spirit. The long dry months that had passed, and how it seemed that nothing good had taken hold inside her and begun to grow. The lifelessness that characterized the climate of her own soul.

Charlotte drove on but did not comment while Beatrice continued to talk about first one thing and then another. She and Dick were remodeling her house to include a Florida room where the deck had been, and she was sure the contractor was stealing their money. Her daughter had left her job and was thinking about starting some computer company. And Beatrice had planned to talk to the committee because she was considering printing a little update for the church cookbook. It seemed that Laura Purvey, from the Baptist Church, had pointed out that some of the recipes weren't clear and that Beatrice thought a little handout or instruction booklet might be helpful.

Charlotte was only halfway listening to the older woman talking on at great length about how Mrs. Purvey had called Beatrice to ask if the milk in the prune cake recipe was supposed to be evaporated milk or condensed milk and that Beatrice had tried both kinds three different times each because she wasn't sure herself. But that she had finally decided that the condensed milk had been right in the first place even if it did make the sauce a little sweet for some folks' taste. And that maybe when the committee met they could consider whether it might be helpful to have a little cookbook guide to go along with the cookbook and what did the pastor think?

Charlotte, not really knowing what the question was, merely nodded a response and mentioned that the hospital parking lot was difficult to find and asked if Beatrice would keep an eye out for the entrance sign. It did halt the conversation as Charlotte had hoped, so that by the time they finally spotted the parking complex, Beatrice had forgotten her idea and was now rambling on about how doctors design hospitals to disorient their patients so they won't notice their bills.

Charlotte agreed that this was actually an intelligent observation and had found that most medical facilities were hard to figure out and that the University Hospital was one of the most difficult. It is long and scrambled, she noted, a series of walkways and buildings that seem to go on for miles. An assortment of old and new treatment areas, it is scattered and loosely connected with signs and arrows but no systematic way of finding rooms. It took Charlotte and Beatrice twenty minutes, outside and in—including two trips back to the information desk and directions from four volunteers, one nurse, and two men in lab coats—before they finally found Nadine's room.

Beatrice asked more people than that, but at least three others she tried to talk to couldn't speak English and another, a doctor in a hurry, only pointed them back to the first entrance near the parking deck. Beatrice was about ready to pick up the emergency phone in the elevator when the two men in lab coats gave them proper directions.

Nadine was on a medical-surgical floor, the fourth, at the end of a short hall near the fire escape. When they walked in, she was propped up, leaning against her pillow, facing the window. Her breakfast tray, untouched and intact, was still sitting on the table in front of her.

"Nadine Klenner, you haven't even taken your morning meal." Beatrice barreled into the room and set her arrangement of flowers on the small side table next to the bed. "You'll have to eat if you want to get your strength back." And she began pulling the lids and plastic off the cups and plates.

Nadine turned toward her visitors. Her face was pale, her eyes dim. She watched as Beatrice rearranged things, trying to make the meal more appetizing.

"Hey Nadine." Charlotte walked around Beatrice to the other side of the bed, in front of the window.

"Hey," she replied softly.

"You know, this stuff is no good," Beatrice said. "Would you like me to get you a hot breakfast?" She peered at Nadine, then at Charlotte as if she could tell her where the cafeteria was.

"I'm not very hungry, Mrs. Newgarden." Nadine pulled herself up a bit in the bed.

"It's Mrs. Witherspoon now, remember?" Charlotte lifted her voice in such a way to try and lighten the mood of Nadine's room, which felt sad and heavy.

Beatrice blushed and rolled her eyes.

"Oh yes, I forgot. You've been married, what? A month now?" Nadine tried to manage a smile.

"Six weeks tomorrow," Beatrice responded. "And no, I'm not pregnant. It's just newlywed weight." She ran her hands across her belly playfully.

"Beatrice and Dick went to the Bahamas for their honeymoon." Charlotte reached in her pocket and fumbled with her car keys.

"And it was too hot to be going there in June," Beatrice said as she slid the bedside table closer to Nadine. "Dick got his head sun-burned the first day, complained the rest of the time because the straw hats hurt him. And nude women?" She threw her hands in the air. "I have never seen so much nakedness!" She picked up the flowers and put them next to the breakfast tray. "I think that's why Dick got burned. Sitting out there at the pool, his brain went soft and his head became a magnet for the sun rays."

Charlotte ignored Beatrice and noticed the cuts and bruises on Nadine's face, the IV stuck and taped to her left hand. Nadine met her eyes and the pastor reached out her hand and touched Nadine's arm.

"How you doing, Nadine?"

Nadine was quiet for a minute before she answered. "Oh, I'm okay, I guess. Broken ribs, ruptured spleen, bruised hip; nothing major." She seemed disappointed.

"What was it that hit you, honey, a yellow cab or a minivan?" Charlotte glared at Beatrice as if she couldn't believe the question. The older woman continued. "Because I've heard both."

Nadine almost laughed. "It was a taxi, Mrs. Witherspoon, but I'm not sure it was yellow."

"Baby, call me Bea, and I know your mama's glad it was only a car because if it had been a minivan . . . well, let's just say, you might not be here to tell us about that." She winked at Nadine and turned to Charlotte, who wasn't sure what to say next but worried that if she didn't say something, Beatrice would keep talking.

"You know, maybe Nadine would like something else to eat." Charlotte was thinking while she spoke. "I bet a milkshake would taste good." She walked around the bed and stood next to Beatrice. "The cafeteria is on the ground floor. If you go back to the elevator, push the button marked G, you should be able to find it. There's a snack bar section and I think you can get Nadine a milkshake."

Quickly, she asked Nadine, "Would you like chocolate or vanilla?"

Nadine was confused. "Um, chocolate I guess."

Charlotte put her arm around Beatrice's waist and walked with her out the door before the older woman could even respond. Then the preacher turned around and came back into the room. But before she said anything to Nadine, Beatrice was behind her. "I'll need my purse," she said without sounding at all like she realized she was being sent away. She picked up her purse and hurried out the door.

Charlotte sighed and closed her eyes, then pulled up a chair and sat down next to Nadine. They smiled at each other, thinking of Beatrice and how she loved to talk. An attendant came in, took the tray from the bedside table, and closed the door behind him. Then there was a long, awkward silence as the two women sat listening to the sounds down the hall and outside but to nothing from inside the room.

Finally, Charlotte spoke. "They treat you okay here?"

"It's all right," Nadine replied. And then another pause. "Some people like this hospital." She nodded while she spoke. "They say it's better than the ones in Greensboro."

Charlotte was at a loss for what to say in response.

"They're all about the same, I think," the patient added.

Charlotte fiddled with the hem of her dress. Someone down the hall was calling for a nurse. She decided not to comment. Construction crews were outside. The men were loud, working somewhere just below the window.

"Your mama visit?" Charlotte already knew Nadine's mother had been at the hospital constantly. That she had been staying at night and still working at her job during the day.

"Yeah. She and my aunts have been here the whole time." Nadine shifted a bit in the bed.

Charlotte wondered about Ray, Nadine's ex-husband. She knew they were having trouble before Brittany died. Nadine's mother had told the pastor before church one Sunday about Ray moving out. She had tried to mention it to Nadine, get her to open up about it; but Nadine didn't act like she wanted to talk about her marriage. She was as closed about that as she was about most things.

Charlotte liked Ray. He had been good with the little girl, and he appeared to care about Nadine. He came to church as much as the rest of the family. Quiet, hardworking, he seemed to be a solid man, one of those who provided for his family while keeping his own desires at bay.

Charlotte remembered thinking after seeing them together one night that they would be able to work things out, that there was enough familiarity and good intention to buoy the marriage, that somehow in the thoughts of leaving and in the realizing of what divorce would mean, they might find enough to stay together. But then the wreck happened and the one person they both loved exactly the same amount, the one event they both knew was the best of life that they had ever been a part of, the child they had created and protected, was gone. And now there was a space between them, wide and noticeable, so that even when they stood near each other, touched, or held something between them to connect them, they remained out of balance somehow. There was just too much broken on each side to bridge them back together.

Charlotte wanted to ask about Ray, if he had been to visit her, if they were still friends, how he was doing with Brittany's death. But it just seemed to be another minefield that perhaps should be avoided in this setting.

Nadine faced Charlotte. "It was her birthday."

Charlotte nodded, startled at Nadine's sudden openness. She waited, then replied. "I know, the day of the . . ." she hesitated, "accident." She finished the sentence.

"Yeah."

Nadine sat up a little in the bed, pulled the pillow up so that it would be situated behind her head. She flinched as she leaned too much to the right side where most of her injuries were. Charlotte stood up to help her; but then Nadine settled on her own.

"I guess you know I did this." Nadine said it quickly, matter-of-factly; and Charlotte returned to the chair without saying anything.

Nadine searched Charlotte's eyes and then looked away. "I guess you think it's a sin." She pushed the pillow down a bit with her good arm.

"I don't think that," Charlotte said easily. "I think it means you're in trouble, that you need some help; but I don't think of it as a sin."

Nadine did not lift her face. She rolled a little toward her left side.

She said, "I worry that she's all alone up there. That she had her birthday and nobody remembered." She brushed her hair out of her face and waited a minute before she continued.

"She loved parties, you know?"

Charlotte smiled, remembering how Brittany had stood up in church one Sunday to announce her party and invite everyone.

"But then I think, how can you have a birthday when you're dead? I mean, what is it to celebrate your being born when you're not alive anymore?"

Charlotte took a deep breath and watched life outside the window. The sun was white and high and the sky was clear. She could see the long crooked arm of a crane lifting steel beams to the roof. She could hear the voices of the workers calling out directions to one another. And she could make out the sounds of traffic on the streets below and the calls of birds that flew above and around everything else that was going on.

She thought Nadine's question was a good one and one that she had never considered. Maybe in heaven or the next life, whatever it is, your birthday is really the day you died, the day you were birthed into another world. Or maybe they do remember the day you were born on earth and you celebrate the time you were there even though the time is over. Charlotte had no idea how to answer Nadine. And she worried that she was disappointing the young woman with her silence.

"That's not really the worst part, though." Nadine followed Charlotte's gaze and stared into the sun. She stopped for some time while Charlotte waited without a word; and then she went on.

"The worst part is thinking about the minutes before she died, how it was for her when the first piece of glass cut her little face. How I did nothing to keep it from her." She reached up and slid her finger down her cheek, across her chin, and then dropped her hand into the sheets.

"Or the moment when she was ripped and thrown from her seat, that second when she knew I wasn't going to defend her. That awful, terrible moment, as quick as it may have been, when she expected me to stop what was happening to her and then knew that I couldn't or wouldn't." Nadine quit talking and the room fell silent again.

Charlotte looked away from Nadine, who lay tormented by what she believed to be a mother's ultimate betrayal, letting her child die, and down into her own lap and began to study her hands. She thought how useless they seemed, held in each other and resting at the roll of her stomach. She unfolded them and spread them out across the tops of her legs, noticing the lines that ran along the knuckles, the veins that crossed and disappeared beneath the tendons. She examined the hairs, the tiny scars, the chipped, splotchy nails.

Charlotte thought about how her hands, like a mother's hands, touched things and held things but how they had never really saved anything or anyone. She turned them over and noticed the blisters on the flaps of skin between her fingers and thumbs and remembered how she had tried to hoe the patch of ground around the parsonage to plant those few flowers but that the ground had been too hard to dig, the grass and weeds too thick. She thought about how she had started with just the desire to have some color around the house, a little garden to plant things, but how her hands had failed to cut through the years of neglect and disarray and how the flowers now were dead in their little plastic trays, thrown somewhere near the garbage can back behind the house.

She remembered how her hands, just like Nadine's hands, had not been able to pump life back into the little girl. How they had not wrestled her own sister from the hold of death. How they had not stopped the coming of evil. They were not able to brush away sorrow. They had not healed or fixed or soothed. And Charlotte just sat there, staring at them as the young woman waited quietly in her bed, and she wondered if God had hands or if he had cut them off after he created the world, watching tenderly but powerlessly as it grew and shaped itself on its own. She wondered if Nadine now hated her hands. Then she curled her fingers into fists and dropped them to her sides, out of sight.

She thought of some things she might say. Things like maybe there was no moment like Nadine imagined; that maybe an angel came even before that split second of impact and with angel hands, sturdy yet gentle, snatched the little soul from her body before there was any pain; that Jesus reached into the car with his scarred and holy hands just before that frightening moment and distracted Brittany from her mother's useless human hands and their inability to save her, and whisked her away to some heaven that makes little girls forget about the things that frighten them and the things they must leave behind.

Charlotte wanted to tell the young mother whose only child was dead that God would not have let the little girl suffer one minute of fear or distress or disappointment; that in that blink of an eye when death came, it was like the light of the sun outside, blinding and quick, and that Brittany passed from this world to the next without even a second of injury.

But the preacher was not sure that this was so; and Nadine didn't act as if she would listen to such words anyway. So she did not speak of hopeful things or mighty things or comforting things. She did not speak at all, and instead her eyes wandered over to the IV stand beside Nadine and the tiny drops of medicine that fell from the distended plastic bag hanging on the pole by the bed. The clear tiny beads that dripped in rhythm into the bloodstream of a woman who wanted to die. Soft little drops that could melt the pain of broken bones and bruised tissue, and that she prayed, but did not believe, might loosen the grip of grief that wrapped around a mother's heart.

She studied the IV as it dangled and dripped and she listened to the whirling of its small motor. Charlotte watched attentively while her empty hands lay limp at her sides, wondering if anything would be able to grow from a heart that seemed so void. How does the womb of a mother of a dead child ever become fertile again? she asked herself. How does life begin, then end, then begin again? How does hope ever bloom without first settling into seed? And how does a pastor offer anything meaningful or comforting or faithful in a world of such senseless and desperate pain? Charlotte struggled with something she might say; but before any words came out of her mouth, there was a noise at the door. Beatrice returned.

"Yoo-hoo," she was calling before she walked into the room.

Nadine wiped her face with the edge of the sheet. Charlotte got up and handed her a tissue.

"I hope you like peach because the chocolate machine was broken." Beatrice came in with two large cups and placed them both on the table. Then she put her purse down by the chair where Charlotte was sitting, pulled two straws out of her pocket, and punched them both into the tops.

"Peach and vanilla. Which one do you prefer?" The older woman was flushed from the walk but seemingly proud that she had been able to deliver what she had been sent to find.

Nadine brushed her bangs away from her eyes. She tried to perk up a bit. "Vanilla," she answered. "Let the preacher have the peach."

"Then vanilla shall be yours." Beatrice wrapped a napkin around the Styrofoam cup and handed it to Nadine.

"We can share this one if you like." Charlotte searched the room for another glass so that she could pour some of the milkshake for Beatrice.

"No, I had a Coke while I was downstairs waiting to see if they could fix the chocolate part."

Charlotte noticed her watch. Although there had not been much of a conversation between the two young women, almost half an hour had passed. She wondered what Beatrice had been doing all that time.

And as if she knew what the pastor was thinking, Beatrice said, "You'll never guess who I saw downstairs." She pulled the other chair up to the bed. She waited but neither woman made a guess. "Clyde Barbee!" She said it with excitement.

Charlotte turned to Nadine, who shrugged her shoulders. She was trying to suck the milkshake through the straw.

"Who's Clyde Barbee?" Charlotte asked as she pulled the top off her cup, stuck the straw in it, and began to stir. Nadine decided to try the same approach.

"You never knew Clyde Barbee?" Beatrice was surprised.

Charlotte shook her head.

"Don't you remember Reverend Barbee?" She looked over to Nadine, who was finally able to taste the vanilla shake. Nadine raised her shoulders again while her mouth was full.

"He was the pastor before the last one." Then Beatrice stopped. "Or maybe before that one . . . I don't remember."

Then she thought about Nadine's young age. "Oh, that's right, he was there before you were born." She turned back to Charlotte. "He married me and Paul." She said this like it would help Charlotte remember him; but the young preacher just dug her straw into the milkshake and pulled it out like a spoon.

"Anyway, he was almost eighty when he left Hope Springs. You can imagine how old he is now."

Charlotte smiled and nodded without having a clue of how old he might be.

"Still visiting the sick," Beatrice said. "And raising some kind of dogs." She stood up and began pulling at her flowers in the vase, lifting them up a bit.

"I don't know what ministry he can do in a hospital, though, because he can't hear a lick. I mean I can't see that he does much good for anyone since I had to scream for him to hear me. Deaf as a door. Can you imagine having somebody come to visit that doesn't listen to a word you say?"

Charlotte lifted her eyebrows and kept drinking the milkshake. It really was quite tasty.

Beatrice tugged at her skirt, pulling it down over her knees. "And mumbles. He just talks so softly I couldn't make out a word he said. I mean, he never talked loud even for a young man. But now? You can't even understand him. So I'm screaming for him to hear me and then screaming for him to speak up. It was some conversation, I'll tell you."

Beatrice just chattered on while Charlotte and Nadine occasionally glanced over at each other and smiled.

Finally, after twenty minutes of Beatrice telling stories about Pastor Barbee, Charlotte licked the last of the peach milkshake from her straw and threw away her cup. She got up and reached over for Nadine's, which was empty as well.

"Well, Nadine, I think it's time for us to go so you can get some rest."

Beatrice saw the clock on the wall and was surprised at the amount of time that had passed. "Oh my goodness, I didn't know it was getting to be this late." She jumped up and pushed both of the chairs against the wall. "Now, these flowers will need a little more water in the morning. Can you remember that or should I ring the nurse and tell her?"

"No, I'll remember." Nadine slid down into her bed. She was tired from the visit. "Thank you both for coming."

Charlotte touched Nadine on the shoulder to say good-bye, but Beatrice walked to the other side, held Nadine's arm, and reached over the woman in the bed to grab Charlotte's free hand. She thought the pastor was going to pray so she bowed her head. Charlotte peered down at Nadine, a bit surprised, but then closed her eyes and led a short prayer.

When Charlotte said amen, Beatrice bent down and kissed Nadine on the cheek. "It doesn't seem like it now," she whispered, "but one day you won't be so sore."

Nadine wondered whether she was referring to the healing of her body or the healing of her heart, but she didn't ask. She preferred to believe Beatrice had known and meant her heart.

Charlotte squeezed her hand. "I'll be back next week." She hoped Beatrice hadn't heard her as the older woman walked around the bed and picked up her purse. Nadine nodded. And the two women left the room, turning back to wave, then discussing which was the easiest way to get back to the parking deck.

Nadine closed her eyes and tried to think of how to explain to her doctor that she had not been absentminded or distracted as she stepped off the curb when the light turned green. That she had not been drunk or stoned. That she had instead been the clearest she had been in months. And because the desire and the intention had been without the influence of drugs or alcohol and had been so plain and obvious, so perfectly sharp, Nadine knew that Charlotte was absolutely right. She was in trouble. And even if the young woman wasn't sure she could find it, she knew she needed help.

She closed her eyes and rolled on her side and pressed her hand to her heart. She felt it beat and rest and wondered to herself if such a thing were possible, that she could ever really want to live again.

Hope Springs Community Garden Club Newsletter

BEA'S BOTANICAL BITS

Pesky Pests

Bugs! Bugs! And more bugs!

There are as many insects and diseases in the plant world as there are in the human one. If you have a garden, be prepared to be aggravated by aphids, Japanese beetles, whiteflies, and cutworms. You may also find mealybugs, leafhoppers, mildew, crown rot, fairy ring, and black spot, just to name a few garden pests. Got a sick plant? You may want to check for bugs.

I suggest you take action before the problem occurs. Keep your soil in top shape. Clean your tools. Inspect plants closely before you buy them. And dispose of anything that might attract or harbor bad bugs.

If some creature has already moved into your garden and started housekeeping, then you have to zap 'em or trap 'em. Insecticides and traps can be bought at your local hardware store, or you can make your own. My favorite is the slug trap, a saucer of beer sunk in the ground. Soapsuds is also an effective remedy to eliminate many pests.

My mama used to kill some insects, stir up their remains, and spray the mixture on the plants. "Bug juice," she used to say. "Even an insect can recognize family."

2

*M*argaret was outside picking off worms and pulling weeds from her flower beds when the call came. She did not hear the ringing of the phone or the message of the nurse who was telling her the news that would change everything for her in the weeks and months ahead. She was yanking out dodder and witch-grass and checking for mites and leaf lice. She was popping the green pods of snapweed, smiling at the quiet explosions that meant more weeds in the future.

She was not a particularly gifted gardener. She had grown up on the farm, worked one most of her adult life, and was most comfortable digging in the earth and nurturing plants, watching them grow. She liked flowers, tried new varieties every year; but she never had a show garden, the kind fancy women like to have people come over to see or the kind where nothing ever grows in them except what was designed on paper and planted in the very beginning.

Unlike many gardeners, Margaret didn't mind some of the weeds that grew. She enjoyed seeing the unique flowers they produced, even if they were just chickweed or gill-over-the-ground. She found the surprises that grew in her garden to be the most interesting. Volunteer sunflowers that heightened her beds and periwinkle that spread across the yard, the things she did not plant, these were the flowers she actually cared for the most.

She gathered up the long tendrils of ivy, the coarse brown stems of Johnson grass, and the sticky stalks of stinging nettle, trying not to let any of them touch the places on her arms, just at her wrists, that remained exposed. It took her three trips with the wheelbarrow to rid herself and her little gardens of all the late-summer growth and the pre-autumn pests. And as she headed back inside, she was pleased with herself for the good work she had accomplished on such a hot August morning.

She walked in and did not notice the blinking light on the answering machine until after she had washed and changed clothes. She saw the indication that a call had come in when she moved away from the refrigerator to retrieve a glass from the cabinet above the sink. She touched the Play button and poured herself some iced tea, not paying much attention as the message began. Then she slid the pitcher back on the shelf and turned to study the machine as the words spilled out.

"Mrs. Peele, this is Linda Masterson at Dr. Morgan's office." The nurse cleared her throat. "Um, we just got back the report from your mammogram and we'd like you to come by sometime this week to talk to the doctor. Call us when you get in and we'll make you an appointment at your convenience." Then there was a click, followed by the instructions on how to save or discard the message. Margaret wasn't sure which to do.

She pulled out a chair and sat down at the kitchen table. She drank her tea and thought a million things. She thought how it could be nothing and how it could be everything. She thought about the nurse, a young woman who must have to make this kind of call every day. She thought about the mammogram and how she and Jessie had gone on the same day last week and how they had celebrated having completed that yearly exam with ice cream at a parlor in Greensboro where they would add a candy bar, cookies, or fruit for just fifty cents extra.

She had decided to have sherbet with tiny slivers of mandarin oranges on top, and Jessie had ordered a butterscotch sundae. They had eaten and laughed and decided that they should have ice cream for more than just the mammogram day and made plans to go again in a month, "just to honor life," Jessie had said.

Margaret thought about her insurance and wondered how much coverage she had for anything serious. She was still a rider on the policy that Luther had gotten from Blue Cross when they first got married. The company had gone through many changes over the years, but she had continued to pay the rising costs and felt sure she had adequate coverage. But she had never tested it herself since she had never had much wrong with her.

She had annual physicals, flu shots, and regular eye doctor appointments. She was careful with her health but fortunate, she knew, because she had never known many physical ailments aside from the customary bouts with viruses and allergies, a gallbladder incident once, and a couple of cases of strep throat. She had never stayed in a hospital, never had surgery, never been sick for more than a few days, and never had anyone take care of her.

She shook her head at the possibilities and decided that before she began making plans for extended care or how to complete insurance claim forms she should see her doctor and hear more about what the mammogram had shown. Margaret got up from the table, called, and made an appointment for later that afternoon. She hung up the phone and walked to the mailbox, resolving not to think about anything until she knew all the facts. But the lingering

questions, the worry, kept her from being very attentive to anything she tried to accomplish for the next few hours.

She went back outside, to the flower bed in the corner behind
the barn, the one with barberry and two butterfly bushes, and read-
justed the railroad ties that bordered it; she reapplied pine straw
and mulch from the bags she kept in the shed. She worked a couple
more hours, trying to focus on matters at hand, trying to notice
and appreciate the long purple clusters that fed so many butterflies,
trying to memorize the sharp angles of the sun; but the anticipation
was overwhelming, the dreaded possibilities just too irresistible. So
she left her outside work, took her shower, and headed for her
appointment. Margaret got to the doctor's office forty minutes
early.

It was not an exam but rather a conversation. She was escorted
into Dr. Morgan's private office and told to have a seat, that he
would be there in just a few minutes.

Margaret took a few deep breaths, remembering the last time
she had sat in front of this desk, waiting to discuss some health-
related matter. It had been almost fifteen years ago when she had
gone to see Dr. Morgan about Luther's stroke, to ask him how it
could have happened to a man so young. She remembered how she
felt, small and lost, and how he had talked to her. He had explained
about the smoking and the genetic factors and the stress of farming; and she had listened respectfully, quietly, but all the time wondering if the doctor believed anything that he said.

It was not that she didn't like Dr. Morgan or that he had a deceit-
ful manner. She had no reason to think that he would lie to her. He
had been their doctor since they had first gotten married, and there
had never been any complaints from herself or Luther. It was just

that on that occasion he seemed nervous in a way that made him appear unreliable, like he was hiding something. He never acted that way during her physicals. He was thorough and asked a lot of questions, polite, interested. But there was just something about having to talk about the death of a patient, the death of her husband, that made him seem edgy, guilty, or at least somehow responsible that Luther had died.

Margaret thought it was an admirable trait for a doctor to be so concerned about his patients, so troubled by their deaths, that he would feel some sense of inadequacy or loss. But she wondered how he ever managed his practice if he took everyone's death so personally.

He knocked and pushed open the door, walked in, and shut it behind him. He was wearing a long white coat over a blue striped shirt and a tie with yellow sun faces on it. Everything was sharp and starched. His pants were navy and his shoes were brown, the leather, though old and worn, now polished and reshaped. Under his arm was a manila file, and he dropped it on his desk as he stopped to shake Margaret's hand.

"Afternoon, Margaret, how are you today?"

They had known each other for more than thirty years, Margaret thought as she stood to greet him. And yet they knew so little about each other. They saw each other only once a year in an exam room, she vulnerable and unclothed, he authoritative and professional. There were so many things he didn't know about her. And there were so many things she didn't know about him. For instance, had he been the father of three children or four? Was his wife still living? Were they divorced? Where was his home? How old was he?

In more than three decades, their relationship had been based entirely upon the results of a blood test and the number of times her heart beat per minute. Strange, she thought, that you can know a person for so long but not really understand anything about him.

"I'm fine, Dr. Morgan." She sat down and dropped her hands in her lap and smiled.

"Had a good summer, I hope."

She nodded. There was very little possibility of her engaging in small talk.

"Well, I know you're nervous about our phone call." He opened up the file and began to read to himself. Then he closed the file, tapped his finger on the edge of his chair, and faced Margaret.

"They've discovered a small mass in your right breast. It's fairly deep, behind the nipple, so I don't expect you've felt it." It was sort of a question and sort of a statement; but he waited for a response. She shook her head.

"Well, we'll take a look before you leave." He took in a breath. His eyes held a certain amount of concern. "Typically, the next step is an ultrasound, to try to locate it more clearly, see if we can tell more about it. I'd like to schedule you for one in the next couple of days. Is that possible for you?"

Margaret nodded.

He saw her worry and continued. "We don't need to think the worst. These kind of results are very common. It could be a false reading, a shadow from movement during the test. It could be a cyst or a fibroid tumor. It could just be some calcification. Doing the ultrasound will help us know a little more."

He peered across the desk at the woman and considered what she might be made of, how she would be in the midst of all the unknowingness, all the uncertainties that were about to be a part of her life. He knew that she had handled her husband's death with dignity and strength, that she had managed all the affairs and remained healthy; but this was different. This had the potential to attack the very core of her being. He wondered what kind of support system she had, what gave her purpose, and how well she could fight trouble.

He had seen a lot of people come and go through his office door. Diagnosis and prognosis, all could be the same, but the difference came in what patients had to take in with them or what they found inside themselves when the real battles began. The ones who opened themselves to the treatments and the hope, they were the ones who almost always survived or had the best odds. The ones who shriveled up and shut themselves off from that which could heal or at least help, they were the ones who never lasted long. He did not know enough about Margaret Peele to know which kind of person she was.

"I would like to do a breast exam, just to see if I can palpate it; but regardless, I will have Linda set up the ultrasound for later in the week."

He wrote something on a piece of paper, an order for the test, Margaret thought.

"Do you have any questions right now?"

There was a pause for a minute while Margaret thought of a hundred questions but did not have the words to articulate them. She wanted to ask what he really thought it was and what she should do to begin preparing for what might be ahead. She wanted to ask how many serious cases start with this same conversation, and out of those conversations and cases, how many of the women were still alive. But she thought they were questions that he might not be able to answer, and she wasn't really sure she even wanted a response.

She shook her head and they both got up. She went into room number 3, undressed, and put on the paper apron that lay folded on the table. It wasn't until after he had completed the exam and told her that he couldn't feel anything and then left her alone in the room that Margaret actually said the word out loud. *Cancer.*

It was not spoken to the doctor or to the nurse; it was not posed in a question or even in an angry bellow. It was not a prayer. She just called out the word like it was a stranger who had simply introduced herself. She said it, took in a breath, exhaled, put her clothes back on, and left the doctor's office.

Margaret pulled out of the parking lot thinking about the word, thinking about what it meant. She remembered her father's struggle with cancer and how the disease crept from organ to organ, silently killing him over a period of long and painful months. She knew of others in her family who died from cancer, a niece, two of her cousins, an uncle who lived out of state. And she wondered if there was some pattern to a family's medical history, some rational way of explaining how cancer, like ants walking to and from their hills, trailed along genetic lines leaving a relative without any means of escape. Or if the malady struck randomly, hitting a person like a stray bolt of lightning. She wondered if she, unlike those whom a bloodline she shared, could survive cancer or whether this bright August day was the beginning of her end.

Driving home, Margaret stopped at the church when she saw Charlotte's car in the parking lot. She got out of her car with the notion that she wasn't going to tell her anything about the test results or her upcoming appointment; she just wanted to see how Nadine was doing.

When she walked in, Charlotte was on the phone.

"I thought the insurance covered this sort of thing."

Margaret stood at the main door as it closed behind her.

"I don't want to go to your person. I prefer to talk to a woman. Your designated clinicians are all men."

Charlotte sounded frustrated, and Margaret wondered if she should wait outside a few minutes. She stayed there a bit longer, trying to decide what to do.

"Fine. When you talk to your supervisor, have them call me. I think I should have some say in this matter. After all, it is my life we're dealing with." Then she hung up the phone.

Margaret walked toward the office. The door was open.

"I didn't think you'd be here this late." Margaret came in and stood near the weeping fig that the pastor kept against the wall. Some of its leaves had dropped, probably because of the air conditioning, and the stems needed to be cut back. But other than that, the plant appeared healthy and she was impressed that the pastor was doing a good job keeping the ficus growing.

Charlotte looked up, surprised that someone was there. When she saw Margaret she relaxed.

"Oh, hi, yeah, well . . ." She stopped and then decided she would go ahead and tell the truth. "I'm trying to make an appointment." She wasn't sure how much she needed to explain. "Insurance requirements," she continued.

She stayed seated at her desk and then noticed that Margaret appeared bothered. Her brow was crossed in worry, something Charlotte rarely saw on Margaret's face.

"What's wrong?" Charlotte asked.

Margaret didn't realize that she was so transparent, and she immediately tried to change the subject.

"Nothing's wrong," she said, almost a little too confidently. She waved her hand in the air and sat down in the chair next to the file cabinet, across from the pastor. "I just wanted to see about Nadine. I'm sorry; I should've called."

Charlotte wasn't sure she believed Margaret, but she went ahead with the line of thinking. "She's okay. I mean, physically, she's banged up pretty bad, but I think maybe she might get some help now. She talked about Brittany. She hasn't done that since it happened."

Charlotte could tell something wasn't right with her friend; but she didn't know what it was or how to ask about it. She shuffled some of the papers on her desk. Margaret watched her.

"How about you?" Margaret asked. "You okay?" She had heard enough of the phone conversation to know Charlotte was needing an appointment with somebody; and even though it wasn't like Margaret to be that nosy, she thought maybe the young pastor wanted to talk.

"Yeah, I'm okay," she said.

Neither of them seemed ready to discuss what was going on with them. There was a pause and then Margaret spoke. Her news blew through the room like a trumpet. It surprised even herself to tell it.

"I have to have an ultrasound. They found something on my mammogram. I just came back from the doctor." She stopped, appearing flustered. She had not expected to share this information so quickly with anyone. She had not expected to speak to Charlotte about it until after she knew something more complete.

Charlotte got up from her desk, stared at her friend, then sat back down.

"I don't know what to say, Margaret."

"There isn't anything to say," Margaret replied. "It's not a big deal." She paused. "I'm fine. Lots of women go to level two."

Charlotte was confused. "Level two?"

"You know, mammogram, level one, ultrasound, level two."

"Oh," Charlotte said. Then she added, "What's level three?"

Margaret hadn't really thought this far. She said softly, "A biopsy, I suppose."

She seemed upset and Charlotte wished she hadn't asked.

"You told anybody else?" Charlotte questioned, remembering that the committee was meeting in just a couple of days.

Margaret shook her head. She lifted her eyes to the bookshelf behind Charlotte's desk. She realized the preacher had changed her office around, moved things a bit.

"I'm sure it's fine," Margaret added, trying to sound convincing.

"Yes," Charlotte replied, unsure of why Margaret had brought her the news. Why wouldn't she tell Jessie or Louise? Charlotte was honored to be invited into such intimacy, but it also rattled her a bit.

"And now you." Margaret had Charlotte in a corner. "What's going on with you?"

Charlotte's face flushed and she started shuffling papers on her desk.

"I'm going to see somebody. To talk to." She felt obligated to tell Margaret since the older woman had shared so openly; but Charlotte was sure she was breaking some sort of rule for ministers.

Rule number 14: Don't tell your parishioners if you've got emotional troubles. Or something like that.

Margaret nodded. "You tell anybody else?"

Charlotte shook her head and thought about the enormity of what they both carried, the next place they had gone in their relationship. She stood up and began putting books on their shelves. She had been studying for her sermon.

"What you preaching on Sunday?"

Margaret knew Charlotte's routine: the preacher read the scripture on Mondays, read books about the scripture on Tuesdays, thought about it on Wednesdays, and wrote the sermon on Thursdays. She knew this because she had asked her once how long it took her to write a sermon and Charlotte had given her the weekly schedule.

"It's from Hebrews," she answered. "The passage about conviction, faith, the middle part." She put up the last book from her desk.

"I was supposed to preach on it a couple of Sundays ago. But we had that guy from the retirement home here."

Margaret remembered the man. He was brash and saucy, a good preacher.

"I started working on it but then put it aside when I knew he was going to be here." She walked around her desk. "But then I figured I'd come back to it." She dropped into her chair.

"You needing to think about faith?" It was a logical question from a parishioner.

"Yeah." She hesitated then asked, "You?"

Margaret fidgeted a bit and smiled. She only nodded.

"Why don't you read me the passage?"

Charlotte slid the Bible from over at her side and flipped to the book of Hebrews. "Now faith is the assurance of things hoped for, the conviction of things not seen. For by it the men of old received divine approval. By faith we understand that the world was created by the word of God, so that what is seen was made out of things which do not appear."

She closed the Bible.

There was a pause and then Charlotte asked, "So what do you think?"

"I think it should make for a good sermon." Margaret leaned back comfortably in her chair. "What do you think?"

Charlotte shrugged her shoulders and thought about what she had learned so far in her studies. That the book of Hebrews was written for an audience of Jewish Christians who were thinking about giving up their newly found faith and going back to their lives as practicing Jews. That scholars thought that the letter was written sometime before the fall of Jerusalem and the ruination of the Temple in A.D. 70. That it was meant to emphasize the superiority of Jesus and to buoy up a confused and lost people's faith. It was a rallying cry to demoralized troops to hold the fort and stay in the fight. And Charlotte thought it was a message she needed to hear but wasn't sure that it was one that she could preach.

"I figure that every once in a while we need to be reminded that we are people of promise." Then Charlotte stopped, put her elbows on the desk, and relaxed her chin into her hands. "Sometimes I have trouble myself remembering what that means."

Margaret studied her pastor and thought how old she seemed to be so young. What was it that had aged her soul so much? What had left her so wanting? The older woman knew about her mother's drinking and her sister's death. Most everyone in the church knew. The family was from around the community and people tended to remember things like alcoholic mothers and young women who die of overdoses. It had, of course, never been discussed. But Margaret wondered if there was something else, something deep in Charlotte's past that, like a parasite in a plant's root system, kept the things she needed to grow from moving up through the channels of her heart.

She wondered if it was merely the preacher's nature to be grievous as she was, burdened. Some people, Margaret knew, were just that way. They just never grew as full or fulfilled as others. And as she considered this, she wasn't sure how people like that ever know if it's just that way for them or if there might be something better in this life.

Margaret was glad that Charlotte was seeking help. And she knew that it had taken a lot on her part to call for a counselor. She hoped that having shared this information with a church member wouldn't discourage her from carrying through with her plans for therapy.

"When's your ultrasound?" Charlotte did not look at Margaret.

"Thursday," she replied.

"Can I come with you?" She knew Margaret wasn't comfortable with this kind of care, but she also knew that she wanted to be with her. She waited for an answer.

Margaret was thinking. She had not considered that her pastor might want to be with her when the next exam was being done. She wasn't sure that she approved of such a thing. She had assumed that she would be alone for this test and for any other test that might follow. What would it mean, she wondered, to have this young woman with her when she got final results?

"I don't know," she replied and then went silent.

Charlotte didn't push. She understood what it was to want to do things on your own. She knew her own streak of independence and wasn't sure herself if she would want someone with her in a doctor's office hearing bad news. It gives people an unfair advantage in a relationship when they know more about things in your life than you know about theirs.

The phone rang and Margaret was glad. She would have a few more minutes to figure out how to respond to the offer.

"Hope Springs Community Church," Charlotte answered professionally.

"Speaking," she said.

The pastor listened to the voice on the other end, wrote down a name on a pad near the phone, and thanked the caller. She said good-bye and hung up.

"Well, I have a name," she said to Margaret. "Marion Gordon," she added.

Margaret didn't know what she meant.

"A therapist," Charlotte said. "They've given me the name of a woman therapist." She stared at the name on the piece of paper.

"You want me to go with you?" Margaret asked, and she didn't mean it as a joke.

Charlotte smiled. "No, I think I can manage this one alone."

There was a pause as a car pulled into the church driveway. Both women followed it with their eyes as it went through to the street behind them.

"It's not the same with your appointment." Charlotte turned the conversation back to Margaret's situation.

Margaret nodded. "I know. I've just not ever done anything like this before. I hadn't thought about having anyone with me." She turned away.

Charlotte knew Margaret's fierceness. She knew that this had unsettled everything for her; and she knew that she wasn't sure what she needed from her pastor at this moment. Maybe she was being intrusive to ask to go along. She wasn't sure of her pastoral impulses anymore, if she ever had been.

"Yes, okay. I'd like you to be there." She took a breath. "But let's not tell anyone just yet."

Charlotte nodded.

"I need to sit with it awhile myself."

Charlotte agreed and did not ask for confidentiality regarding her own circumstances. She knew that was understood.

Margaret got up from her chair. "It's at 8:30 on Thursday morning." She dug her keys from her purse. "That's not too early for you, is it?"

Charlotte shook her head. "You want to meet me here, or should I come to your house?"

"No," Margaret walked toward the door. "Here is good. I'll meet you at 8:00."

She reached for the doorknob, then added, "Thank you."

"Margaret," Charlotte replied, "thank you."

The two women said good-bye and Charlotte sat again in the chair behind the desk. She flipped open her Bible and read once more the words from the book of Hebrews.

Then she pushed the Bible away from her and leaned back in her chair.

"I don't know," she said to God or herself or to whoever she thought might be listening. "How is there assurance of something when you don't even know what you need to be assured of?"

She put her hands behind her head and stretched her feet far under the desk. The only sounds she heard were Margaret's car pulling away from the church and the lonely way the office settled after someone had left.

She stared at the ceiling, the light brown stain where water had puddled and dried just above her head, and then dropped her eyes to the plant by the door. It was tough, she thought. It had withstood moves and climate changes and not enough sun. It was potbound, roots drawing up over the edges. And even though the person selling the plant to her had told her that it was meant to grow that way, it still seemed abnormal to Charlotte. It was bottomheavy, tangled, pushed within itself so that it was stunted, kept from growing as tall, as full as it could be.

The leaves were bright green and wide, but many were wilting and falling. A small spider crawled along a stem. Charlotte stared at the plant and then closed her eyes. How does a person lift herself above the sadness? she thought. What can pull a heart straight beyond itself?

She picked up the receiver and dialed the number she had only recently received. Her first appointment was scheduled for the following week.

Hope Springs Community Garden Club Newsletter

BEA'S BOTANICAL BITS

A Dirty Subject

Girls, let's talk dirty. Have you checked the soil in your garden lately? Are your tomatoes getting dry rot, or are your pepper plants not as sturdy as last year? Then maybe you need to put a few strips of newspaper around the roots or buy a little fertilizer. Check the nitrogen level and add a bit of lime.

Soil content affects the nature of your produce. My cousin, who lives near the coast, swears that watermelon is sweeter there because the sandy soil is more sugary than our claylike dirt here. But I wouldn't know about that.

You can always spice up your dirt with what is delicately referred to as "cow tea." I'm talking manure, sisters. And don't act offended. You know a little dung goes a long way.

Good soil is the most important key to growing a bountiful and healthy garden.

"As the president of the Women's Guild..." Beatrice wanted to get the meeting started so that she could show her honeymoon pictures.

"Beatrice Newgarden Witherspoon, if you don't shut up with that call to order, I'm going to announce to the church that you had sex before you got married." Louise pushed her way onto the sofa and flopped down next to Jessie.

Charlotte laughed.

Beatrice rolled her eyes and opened up the box that held her pictures. She began sorting the small albums so that she could keep the trip in photographic sequence.

Even though the cookbook had been completed months ago, the committee continued to meet. Working on the cookbook, Beatrice had discovered that she enjoyed writing. And since she had always loved to garden, the Garden Club newsletter seemed like the next perfect project. But she couldn't seem to say good-bye to the women from the committee.

Beatrice kept calling her friends together even after the cookbook manuscript was finished and sent to the printer. She manufactured reasons why they had to meet until finally Jessie recognized what she was doing and suggested that they simply come together once a month, just to talk, stay connected. It was a welcomed idea, and Beatrice was only too glad not to have to make up reasons to keep calling everyone.

They met at each woman's house, rotating the schedule. The hostess was in charge of refreshments, though they didn't expect or desire anything too elaborate. Tonight they were at Jessie's. She had some leftover pound cake and a few strawberries, coffee and lemonade. It was quiet in the house since Lana and Wallace had gone out to dinner, the baby was sleeping, and James Senior was out back working on his car. Everyone had arrived, and Beatrice was getting impatient. She decided to go ahead and show her pictures even though the women were still talking to each other.

"This set is from Miami," she began, clearing her throat. She handed the little plastic album to Charlotte. The women settled down. "We stayed the first night here and then got on the boat the following morning."

There were pictures of the desk clerk smiling, standing behind a tall wooden counter. A blue fish hung above her head. There were pictures of the lobby, wide and tropical with palm trees and tall, lacy ferns. There were shots of Dick unpacking in the room, the room service table with breakfast, Beatrice shopping for suntan lotion in the hotel sundries shop, and a couple of pictures of the bathtub, which was big enough for four people.

Charlotte then passed them on to Louise, who was not at all interested. Here were twenty-four pictures of a hotel and the first night. It was going to be a long meeting. She finished and passed the album to Jessie, who passed it on to Margaret, sitting in the chair beside the sofa.

"Now these are from the boat before we sailed." Beatrice had been waiting for this opportunity for more than two weeks. She had taken two cameras, one that took wide-angle shots and the other just a simple point-and-shoot. She was pleased with how the pictures had turned out and excited to share her photographic adventures.

"There are two different pictures of each shot." She proudly passed them to her pastor.

Charlotte turned quickly through the pages, passing them to Louise, who now didn't even bother to look. She sat near Jessie so that it appeared they were seeing the photographs together.

There were pictures of people waving from the port up to the passengers on the ship, pictures of Dick and Beatrice arm in arm, pictures of seagulls and the pool and the ocean, and lots of shots of Dick studying things, the itinerary, the instruments on the front end of the ship, the menu in the dining room, and the list of costs of services. He seemed particularly engrossed in this piece of literature. His brow was crossed and he was chewing on his lip.

Beatrice rambled on as she handed the albums to Charlotte, who quickly flipped through the pictures and gave them to Louise.

"What are you doing here, Bea?" Jessie was more polite than Louise.

It was a photograph of Beatrice standing behind the captain, one hand waving to Dick, who was obviously taking the picture, and the other hand hidden behind the man's body. She had a strange smile on her face as she stood against the side of the ship.

"Oh, that's Captain Mike. He was greeting the other passengers." She fumbled through the albums. "He had the cutest butt." She went on. "I mean, the way his white jacket fell right at the rounded part. And his uniform pants were kind of tight." She motioned with her hands the line of the man's body. "It was real sexy, and Dick bet me that I wouldn't touch it."

Margaret turned to Jessie, surprised. But it was Louise who asked, as she pulled the album back toward her so that she could see the picture for herself, "You grabbed a man's ass?"

"Well, not grab exactly, just handled." Beatrice couldn't see why the women appeared so shocked.

Jessie and Margaret shook their heads. Charlotte got up from her seat to peer over Louise's shoulder at the picture.

"Beatrice, you actually touched the captain's rear end?" After Charlotte sat down, Jessie passed the album on to Margaret so that she could see the photograph for herself.

Beatrice sighed. She took a sip of her coffee and put down the cup. "I don't see what the fuss is all about. I handle dead people's butts all the time. And besides, there were a lot of folks around. I hardly think he figured out that I was intentionally rubbing him."

She saw no reason for this conversation and wished she had removed that particular shot from the little album. She hadn't thought anyone else would notice that she wasn't just smiling and waving at the camera.

Jessie reached for a bit of her cake. "Girl, you are something."

"Beatrice, did the captain know you fondled him?" Charlotte couldn't believe what she was hearing.

"Beatrice, it doesn't seem so crowded to me." Margaret was studying the picture. "Are you sure he didn't realize what you were doing?" She handed the album to Beatrice, who had passed another one to Charlotte, who was waiting for the answer to Margaret's question.

She held the album in her hand, thinking, then replied, "Well, he did seem a little, oh, I don't know, nervous around me for the rest of the cruise."

She examined the picture again, remembering the occasion. "We never got asked to sit at the captain's table for dinner."

Louise made a funny noise, like a grunt.

"I just thought it was because Dick wore the same tie every night."

Jessie got up to get more coffee for everyone. "Beatrice, you cannot sit there and tell me you thought it was all right to touch another man's butt in public! I know you are not that naive."

She walked into the kitchen, then returned to the room.

Beatrice smiled and put the box of pictures down by her chair. She took a little more coffee from Jessie. "Oh, all right," she confessed, "I was a little nervous when I did it. But I did get a hundred dollars from Dick." She said this proudly. "And that counts for a lot because that man doesn't part with his money all that easy."

Louise handed the next album to Jessie. She hadn't even seen the pictures. She turned her attention to her friend sitting next to her. "So what's going on with you and the old man?" she asked.

"What do you mean?" Jessie replied. She was flipping through the pictures from the second day of the cruise, and she was glad that Beatrice had quit passing more albums.

"I mean, why is he fixing up his car? He isn't leaving again, is he?"

Margaret shifted so that she could see out the kitchen window into the backyard. James was standing on a crate, bending over the engine.

Jessie ate the rest of her cake. "He's got a leak," she replied hesitantly, "somewhere in the oil line."

No one said anything, and the room was quiet except for the clinking of forks on plates, cups on saucers. Louise simply stared at Jessie while she finished her dessert.

"What, Louise?" She pulled her body around so that she was facing the woman sitting next to her on the couch.

"I'm asking you what," Louise said.

The other women were silent.

Jessie took in a breath and held up the thermos with the coffee in it. It was a question if anyone wanted more. Everyone shook their heads. She poured herself another cup and stirred in the milk. Then she sat down on the sofa and began.

"James isn't sure he wants to stay here." She said this calmly, as if it were a weather report or the mention of some known event.

The women glanced around at each other, surprised at the comment, stunned at the news. James and Jessie had been together again now for a number of months, ever since their grandson's wedding. They, like everyone else in the community and the family, thought he was staying for good, thought he had come home, landed safely back in the cradle of his heart.

"What do you mean he doesn't want to stay here?" Louise was angry. She had sat up on the edge of her seat.

"He's bored. I don't know. He said he was tired of the city, that he wanted to be back here, in the country, with me. But I don't know; he's just restless." Jessie stopped.

Margaret dropped her head. She knew what this meant for Jessie.

"This place . . ." She stopped again. "It's just got a lot of bad memories for him."

Jessie got up, stacked up everyone's plates, and walked with them into the kitchen. Still no one spoke.

"So, take a trip," Beatrice offered. "It's amazing what a nice vacation can do for your frame of mind. You can take a cruise or go to the beach. Why don't you go on and retire from that old mill you're still working at and the two of you take off for a couple of months somewhere?"

She put her napkin in her coffee cup and eased down in her chair. She thought it was a perfect solution. On their honeymoon, Dick had relaxed altogether into a different man. He was even considering selling the funeral home to one of the corporations that were starting to buy up all the family businesses. She was sure this was all James Senior needed.

Charlotte waited as Jessie walked back in the room. She sat slumped in her seat. "Jessie, maybe that's not such a bad idea. Could you take some time together?"

Jessie smiled. "Well, funny you should mention that," she said as she sat down next to Louise and threw her arm up over her. "I've decided to retire."

Louise nodded in approval and Margaret touched her on the leg. Beatrice clapped her hands lightly together.

"Good for you, Jessie," Margaret said. "You've been there a long time."

"Lord yes, you've stayed with that mill family a whole lot longer than I was able to." Louise moved so that she could see Jessie without straining her neck. "And now they got the boy in charge. How do you put up with that snotty-nosed college boy as your boss?"

Jessie laughed. "Oh, he ain't so bad." She turned to Beatrice and said, "I just remind him that I'm someone who changed his diapers and whipped his butt."

Beatrice seemed pleased at this.

"And then he just dismisses himself out of my office and leaves me to do my work."

Margaret stacked the other photo albums on the coffee table and took her last bit of coffee. Then she wiped her mouth with her napkin. "That's just wonderful, Jessie. When's your last day?"

Before she could answer, James Senior walked in through the kitchen. He stopped at the door as the women were laughing, engaged in cheerful conversation.

"Well, what has made the committee so happy this evening?" He grinned at them and winked at his wife.

"Jessie's just told us the big news that she's retiring." Charlotte spun around in her seat so that she could see James.

"Yes, and we're trying to decide where you should go in celebration," Beatrice added.

James leaned against the door frame. "Well, I guess she told you that we're planning to move out west." He did not realize the conversation hadn't gotten that far. "We're planning to celebrate the rest of our lives."

The room was still. Not one of the women moved in her seat or turned to face Jessie. They just stayed that way, staring at James as he suddenly understood that they had not been told that part of the family's plans.

Finally Margaret spoke. "Moving? Jessie, you're going to move?"

Jessie dropped her head. She had not known how to tell her friends that she and James Senior were considering a move to California. She wasn't sure of what it would mean or how they would take it. She waffled between thinking that it wouldn't be a big deal, that they really weren't that close, and worrying that it would be more difficult to leave than she might imagine.

She knew that these women had become her family; and when

James began to talk about moving, began pulling out pictures and books about northern California and the possibilities for them, she thought it was just a means to make her laugh. She merely played along with what she thought was only daydreaming. Then the conversations and the potential for moving became more real. And truthfully, she liked the thought of cleaning out her life, scaling down, and starting over in a new place. She found the idea exciting and began to let an old dream start to breathe.

She had loved it when she first left home for college. She loved learning a new city, meeting the new people, having the new experiences; and she never thought when she was younger that she would come back to Hope Springs. But Jessie soon learned that life rarely moves in the direction one first imagines. And before she knew it, thirty years had come and gone and she was still only five miles from the place where her life began.

Before James's homecoming and before the spilling out of his old dreams, Jessie thought it was too late for her to think about a new move, a change, a new address. She figured she had aged out of the adventuresome life phases. She knew what her life was, and for the most part she was happy with it. She kept Hope and provided for Lana and Wallace while they were trying to get their feet on the ground. She didn't mind her work so much. She had other family close by. She had become settled; and she loved this group. These women. And there was this part, this surprising part—these women were harder for her to consider leaving than even her beloved grandchildren.

When Jessie began to make excuses about not being able to leave, James had not understood her friendships, causing the biggest fight they had had since his return. He said that he could appreciate not wanting to leave family or a home, that even he had mixed feelings about leaving James Junior alone to work in the fields and Wallace and Lana, who now would have to fend for themselves, but four white women? he asked. One of them gay, another one just plain meddlesome, and another one younger than their children—well, this was simply beyond his comprehension. Margaret, he knew, was a good friend. She was reliable, sensible, and compassionate. But, he had told his wife, Margaret could visit often, stay as long as she liked. After all, he had added, she was alone, didn't have family; maybe she'd like to move with them. But the other three he had questioned: had they really gotten that close?

Jessie was mad at him for what he said, but she had stumbled on that. She remembered that she had never had many friends growing up. She was always too busy to nurture relationships. With lots of chores to do at home, parents who maintained strict order, and her studious ways, there was very little time for a social life. When Jessie went to college, she met James early, so that any friends she had were always second priority to that primary relationship. It wasn't until now that she really felt as if she knew what it meant to have a friend. And she then realized that she had four. And these four were at least dear enough to have to give it a lot of thought before leaving them.

"Understand or not," she had told her husband in anger, "these women fill me up. And it's going to take me a little time before I can just say good-bye and leave." And James had backed down, careful not to bring it up again.

Margaret was waiting for an answer. The other women now stared at her.

"Yes," she answered seriously, "James and I are planning to move to Oakland. He has a sister out there who'd like us to buy the place next to her." She moved around a bit, readjusting her position next to Louise.

"Jessie, how long have you been thinking about this?" Margaret knew this was a question everyone had on their minds.

James left the room, quite sure that he was never going to hear the end of this from his wife. He walked out without anyone even noticing that he had gone.

"We started talking about it earlier this summer," Jessie said. "At first, I didn't think anything of it. But then, I don't know, I figured it would be fun." She tried to sound excited.

"When?" Charlotte just asked the one-word question.

"We don't know yet."

"Well, what are we talking about here?" Louise probed. "Fall, winter, next year?" Her voice was sharp, clipped.

"I don't know," Jessie said again.

Charlotte turned to Margaret, wondering if she was going to tell her news as well. Margaret rubbed her hands up and down her legs and shook her head as an answer. Beatrice noticed the exchange, curious about what secret they shared.

"Well, I don't see how you could move before next year." Beatrice decided against asking Margaret what was going on and spoke to Jessie. "I mean, you have to retire, you'll have to clean out everything, you have to pack and get everybody settled. So that the earliest you could really leave is December, and you know you don't want to move in the cold."

Beatrice seemed to have it all figured out. At least if they knew it wasn't going to be anytime soon that Jessie was moving, they could clear the air of this heaviness and she could share more of her photographs.

"Did you see the shots from when we went snorkeling?" She dropped her hands to her side and picked up the box again.

"Beatrice, we don't want to see any more of your pictures. Frankly, the thought of seeing Dick in a bathing suit is more than I can take right now." Louise tugged at the front of her shirt. "I can't believe you've been thinking about this for three months and have not mentioned it to us." She was hurt at Jessie's silence.

The other women dropped their eyes. They felt the same way. Margaret, especially, felt a sense of betrayal that Jessie had not spoken of the possibilities. Hadn't they just been together last week at the mammogram? Why hadn't Jessie said anything then? And then she realized her own secret and figured that she had no room to make judgments.

"I'm sorry," Jessie said. "I was still trying to get used to the idea myself." She paused. "I like the idea of moving somewhere else. But it was hard thinking about telling anyone."

Charlotte didn't know what to say. She was as surprised and disappointed as the other women. Jessie was very dear to her. She was the voice of reason in the congregation, a person, like Margaret, that she knew would always find and tell the truth. She was solid, strong, and resilient. She held that community together; and Charlotte couldn't imagine being in the church without her.

"Well, I think this is horseshit." Louise was the only one not letting Jessie off the hook for her decision and her silence. And because these women knew Louise and loved her for who she was, even Jessie was not put off by her bluntness. "You've been considering this the entire summer and you haven't let on, haven't asked us what we thought, haven't wanted our opinions. Well . . ." She stammered a bit. "I just think that's horseshit."

Still, the room was quiet.

Jessie faced her friend sitting beside her. "Okay, Louise, tell me what you *really* think about me moving."

Louise didn't skip a beat. "I think it's horseshit. You let that man come back into your life after he walked out on you, and now you're just going to take up everything and follow him to California?" She was not to be stopped. "Suppose he gets bored out there, then what are you going to do?" She hoped for some help from Beatrice and Margaret, but they were silent.

"Horseshit," she said one more time.

"He's my husband, Louise. I love him. And I'm not doing this because he wants me to. Sure, it was his idea. But I very much like the idea. I've never wanted to stay here."

These words stung and the women showed as much.

Jessie realized how that sounded. "I don't mean it like that. I love you all. I love this house and my community. But I'm not at home here either. I like to travel. I've always thought I'd move somewhere else, but then there were the kids and Mama and Daddy to take care of. I want to experience life in another place before I die. I want to go with him. But I also just want to go."

Even Beatrice felt a certain twinge of pain that friendship couldn't keep Jessie from making this decision. The women were left empty. The news sucked and drained them. They tried to appear understanding, tried even to appear happy for their friend—everyone but Louise. She had decided that Jessie's choice was a choice against her, and she wanted nothing to do with being polite and gracious. She got up and started to leave.

"Well, I for one don't need to hear any more. This hurts me, Jessie, and I'll just have to be hurt for a little more before I can be nice."

She made an exit before anyone tried to stop her. All four watched as Louise stormed out the door, and then they listened as she pulled out and drove away. An awkward silence followed.

"Horseshit, huh?" Jessie asked the other women. "That what you think too?"

Margaret forced a laugh. "It's hard news to hear, Jes. You're like a sister to her, to all of us."

Jessie nodded without saying anything else.

"Well, look at the time!" Beatrice jumped up. "I have a husband of my own and he'll be waiting for me." She moved in front of Jessie. "I'll help you however I can." She reached out her hand. "And don't worry about Louise; she'll come around. I mean, she might not be pleasant, but she won't stay mad."

Jessie stood up and hugged Beatrice. "Don't forget your pictures."

"Oh, right." She returned to her seat and grabbed up the box. "Unless, does anyone want to keep them?"

Margaret and Charlotte both shook their heads. Jessie waved her hands before her, a negative gesture.

"Oh, okay. Then we meet next month at Margaret's, right?" She turned to Margaret.

Margaret nodded.

"All right then. I'll see everyone on Sunday." And she bounced out the door.

"I guess I should go too," Charlotte said as she got up from her seat. She walked into the kitchen and set her coffee cup and saucer on the counter behind her. "I can't believe this, Jessie." This was all she could say as she walked back into the room where the other women waited. She hugged her friend and then turned to Margaret. "You coming?"

Margaret shook her head. "I want to talk a bit to Jessie."

Charlotte nodded and headed toward the door. She turned around and said, "Tell James I said goodnight."

"Yes," was Jessie's response. The young pastor left. She went to her car and sat down, but she did not leave.

Jessie began cleaning up. She wasn't sure what kind of reprimand she was about to get from her friend.

"Jessie, please, sit down." Margaret remained in her seat.

"Margaret, I'm sorry. I should have told you," she said as she went back to the sofa. "I just . . ." She stammered a bit. "I just . . . it's just harder than I thought. I couldn't bring myself to tell you." She dabbed at her eyes with a tissue.

Margaret reached over and they held hands. "I know," she said.

There was a pause until they heard James moving things around in the back bedroom.

"That man!" Jessie said in exasperation. "His big mouth, and now if he wakes that baby!" She got up to leave, but Margaret held her hands tighter.

"Wait," Margaret said. "I have something I need to tell you too."

Charlotte watched through the window from her car as Margaret told the news to Jessie. She knew she shouldn't be spying like that, but she had been so curious about what Margaret was going to do. After the ultrasound and then the biopsy and hearing the doctor's recommendations, Margaret had decided to tell the group tonight. She was scheduled for surgery in two weeks.

The outcome could not be certain at this time. But the size of the lump, the positive reading from the biopsy, and the results from the blood test from her earlier appointment all seemed to point to cancer. Although they could move more conservatively and just do a lumpectomy, the radiologist, the surgeon, Margaret, and her doctor concurred that a mastectomy was really the best way to go. They were hopeful that with its early detection and removal, they could isolate and eliminate any more signs of the disease. They had all agreed this was the best route to take.

Charlotte had sat in the room with Margaret as all the reports were read. She reached for and held Margaret's hand at one point. But she felt incomplete, fragmented; and she had told Margaret so. "The others should have been with us," she had said to Margaret, who had nodded in agreement. And they both decided at that point that, for the rest of the way, Margaret would let the other women be a part of the process.

Jessie sat back at first and then dropped to her knees in front of Margaret. Then Charlotte watched as Jessie pulled Margaret out of her own chair and into herself, and they stayed like that for a very long time.

The young woman folded her arms around the steering wheel. She wept while she watched two women, two friends, fall into each other and into the sadness and into the fear and the sorrow. She saw them rock and sit and wipe the tears and hold each other some more.

It was powerful, she thought, what women bring to each other in calamity. It may not be forceful or disciplined or organized. It may not solve anything or provide a linear direction for others to follow. It may not have the intensity or action that men's responses often have. On the surface it might even appear sparse or meager, insignificant, small. Many will pass right over it, never even recognizing its strength. But Charlotte knew it to be what it was. It was the place from which everything else grew. It was rich and fertile, the foundation of life. It was the bedrock of faith, but one she knew she did not have when she had sat in the hospital room with Nadine. And she wished she could have offered what these women seemed to possess.

Having witnessed enough, the young pastor started the car and pulled out into the night.

Hope Springs Community Garden Club Newsletter

BEA'S BOTANICAL BITS

Let There Be Light

God said it; so it must be so! Give your plants the sun. Still, a gardener must use some discretion. After all, sunshine is like wine. Some folks can take only a little.

You can tell if a plant needs more light because it will be dwarfed and put out only a few leaves. Also, sun-starved plants will lean in the direction of the light and have long shoots. On the other hand, if there's too much sunshine, the leaves will turn brown and appear burned.

Learn about the light needs of your plants before you put them in your garden. But remember, plants are like children: every day they need quality time in the sun.

4

*C*harlotte drove up the street slowly. Marion Gordon's office in downtown Greensboro was on a shaded street where homes had been turned into workplaces for psychologists, non-profit agencies, even a few lawyers. Close to the hospital, adjacent to a city park, the tree-lined street was traveled by pedestrians, cyclists, and automobiles, all hurrying along to someplace else.

The office was on the corner, flanked by large oaks and rows of bushes that grew bulky and green. The house number was printed on a sign that hung beneath the mailbox at the curb and was also painted in black just above the front door, which faced the main thoroughfare.

Charlotte pulled into the driveway slowly and parked behind the house where Marion Gordon and the other therapists had their sign. The small gravel lot was discreet, noticeable only if you were watching for it, and it appeared to be shared by the therapists and the women's center housed in the building next door.

Gordon was a social worker associated with a group whose services included individual, marriage, and family therapy, with an emphasis on childhood trauma and abuse. Charlotte found this out by looking them up on the Internet, where their web page was filled with pictures of happy children playing together and phone numbers flashing at the bottom of the page for domestic violence hot lines. After reading it, she considered telling her insurance

company that she had changed her mind and would rather go
ahead and see one of their men. She was not, after all, interested in
returning to her childhood, wading through all the memories, all
the forgotten disappointments. And even though she did not try to
fool herself into thinking she had lived a perfect childhood, she had
not ever considered herself abused.

The property was fenced on three sides with tangles of soft-
stemmed clematis and climbing rose twining in and out of the thick
wooden rails that separated lawn from lawn. There were ever-
green trees planted in the corners, one cedar, the other a fir, and
large rocks placed at the base of their trunks.

Charlotte shut off the engine and waited. She thought about
going back home. She considered that she did not have to go
through with this and maybe all that she really needed was a good,
long nap. She thought about her parishioners and considered how
they would react if they knew she was seeing a therapist. She
thought about her mother, Joyce, how many times she had gone to
see counselors, AA sponsors, rehab specialists, and remembered
how much of that work had been useless.

After Serena died, Joyce had tried numerous times to get her
daughter to go with her to see a counselor. But the older woman
was still drinking at the time and Charlotte had refused. Years later,
when Joyce had been sober for a few years, she had suggested therapy again. But as before, Charlotte hadn't been interested.

Even now, having decided on her own, Charlotte was unsure
about coming. She wondered what good it could do, how much it
would really help, if there was really any way to discover the
source of her discontent. And yet, she felt that it was the right thing
to do. It wasn't as if she saw herself as being at her wit's end or

clutching her final straw. She simply realized that the time felt right and that if she was going to be able to be of much help to anyone else, she had to start understanding the condition of her own heart and figuring out how she might help herself.

Reluctantly, Charlotte got out of her car and walked toward the building. Off to the right, facing the side street, ivy draped the top of an arbor marking the entrance to a small garden, which was hemmed in by thick shrubs and tall clumps of grass. The garden had a bench, a few cement sculptures, and thin clusters of late summer flowers and more large rocks. It was a vista of steadiness, clarity, completely, Charlotte noted, unlike the landscape of her mind.

She peeked through the foliage where butterflies floated above and noticed inside a green stone angel, her face dropped down, her wings draped about her. Three mosaic steps, topped with brightly colored pieces of cut glass, led to the bench. Since the young woman was a bit early for her appointment, she stepped inside and sat down. She listened to the hum of bees, the muffled sounds of traffic nearby, the silence in between all the natural and unnatural noises, and thought about an angel who had dropped her face from the light.

She bent to see the angel's eyes, to understand whether this had been a posture of prayer or a gesture of resignation; but she was unable to see the angel's face clearly. Charlotte realized that to see the angel completely she would have to get down on the ground on her knees. And since she decided that she wasn't curious enough to risk getting dirty, she sat back on the bench and glanced up. The wind danced through the branches of an old flowering ash that had been planted in the yard next door but was draping and leaning across the garden and even out into the parking lot. The sun appeared and disappeared through the limbs, and Charlotte took in a deep breath.

She closed her eyes and let herself relax. She felt hidden and secure within the green walls and the tall twisting ceiling. It was a peaceful place, this little garden planted behind a therapist's office, and she liked the way it was shaded and light, both at the same time. She sat, remembering the places she played when she was a child, the tall trees that she climbed and stayed in for hours, swinging between the branches, pretending she was flying above the earth. She recalled the empty creek bed where she kept a blanket and smooth river stones, the place she thought of as her sacred space, though at that time she would never have had those words to describe it.

Charlotte sat in this small, leafy room and was driven to the times and places when she was a little girl and had found solace along the trunks of great trees, a time when she had run to the forest in anger or fear and emerged from the woods stronger, more confident.

It had been the strength of the tall Virginia pines and the grace of mountain laurel and sweeping sugar maples, the stirring of breezes and the cacophony of animal sounds, the cool mossy ground and the lacy webs of spiders that calmed her and quieted her and put her heart back in place.

She sat there, restful and remembering, drawn into neatly carved hours of her girlhood when she had found and claimed all the help she needed. Here in those memories of clean and untroubled moments, here in the chambers of wood and vine, leaf and flower, she remembered feeling alive and lively. Here, Charlotte thought, here surrounded by nature is the best place I have ever been.

The young pastor feasted in her memories until she was pulled back hard into the present. Someone drove right up to the arbor, skidded to a stop on the gravel, got out, and slammed the car door shut. Charlotte, jolted, jumped up and looked at her watch. It was time for her appointment.

She followed the woman who had just arrived from the parking lot to the office. The woman was bottom-heavy and broad and walked with a certain amount of difficulty. She moved slowly, blowing puffs of air with every few steps. She had a few folders and papers under her arm, a black purse swinging from her elbow, and she was balanced only by the way she dropped her weight from side to side.

Charlotte stayed a ways behind so as not to startle her but was still able to overhear the woman as she mumbled under her breath something about "egomaniacs" and "self-absorbed losers." Charlotte assumed that she was a client for one of the other counselors in the house. The woman, stomping and puffing, moved in through a side door and pulled it shut behind her. Charlotte walked around to the front.

It was an old house, recently refurbished with a new coat of stark white paint and orange-red shutters and window boxes filled with fat marigolds and thick purple and yellow pansies. The front porch was surrounded with hanging baskets of ferns, and large green rocking chairs stood side by side, five or six in a row. It was homey and welcoming, like a bed-and-breakfast or a grandmother's house, Charlotte thought as she went in through the front door. The first room was wide and cool; and since the air conditioning was on and working, the windows were closed and bolted. And as soon as Charlotte closed the door behind her, everything was quiet.

The room was decorated in bold solid colors, with light billowing fabric thrown across curtain rods on the top of each window. It was lively and sunny in the room, cheerful. Charlotte thought it was possible that a psychological assessment had been done for each aspect of the decorating of the therapy house. She wondered if all the counselors met to discuss which colors were therapeutic, which ones created more of a healing space, or if they just told a decorator to make it as happy as possible.

There was one woman sitting in a chair on the right side. She was facing an empty desk just at the hall entrance. The woman didn't glance up from her magazine, and Charlotte sat down on the opposite side of the room, on a large brown sofa, waiting for someone to arrive at the desk and tell her what to do.

In a few minutes a middle-aged man, tall with thinning hair, came into the room from the back and motioned for the woman sitting and reading the magazine to follow him. He did not speak or even appear to notice Charlotte. The two of them chatted down the hall about the weather, and the woman seemed comfortable with him as they went around a corner and disappeared. Charlotte looked at her watch. It was five minutes past her scheduled appointment. She considered wandering around and trying to find somebody, just to make sure that she was in the right place. But then she decided that she should probably just stay out in the waiting area for a little while longer.

She studied the room. There were overstuffed chairs with lots of pillows. Pots of flowers stood in every corner, and piles of magazines covered the coffee table and spilled onto the floor next to the seats. There was a wall with long narrow bookshelves behind her, but she didn't turn around to see what books were there. The air conditioner blew back on and Charlotte looked at her watch again. A few more minutes had passed.

Finally, just as she was deciding to leave, Charlotte heard a door open down the hall and the sounds of someone coming toward the waiting room. She strained her neck to see who it might be; but as soon as she heard the puffs and the heavy steps, she knew it was the same woman she had followed in.

"You Charlotte Stewart?" She stared directly at Charlotte. Charlotte nodded.

"Then, come on with me." And the broad woman turned and walked back in the direction from which she had come.

Charlotte got up and hurried after her. The woman pushed opened a door into an office and stood behind it while Charlotte walked in. Then she shut it and locked it. She sat down in a chair by a desk and pulled out some forms and tried to find a pen. She gasped and sighed the entire time.

Charlotte stayed near the door, feeling a little unsure of what she should do.

"Can't ever find something to write with." The woman fumbled in her desk drawers and along the top under folders and papers.

Charlotte reached in her purse and handed a pen to the therapist. She smiled and took it and started to write something on one of the forms, then threw the pen and the papers down in front of her. "Well, why don't we just talk first? Go on and have a seat." And she motioned toward a sofa that was pushed up against a window.

She got up as Charlotte walked over and sat on the couch. Then the woman plopped down in a chair situated across from the minister.

"I'm Marion," she said, finally introducing herself.

"I'm Charlotte," was her response as she brushed down the front of her dress a bit nervously.

"Your insurance company called me last week. I never heard of them." She pulled herself up a little higher in her chair.

"It's a denominational company." Charlotte paused, then decided to explain. "I'm a pastor and we have our own insurance company."

The woman nodded as if she understood. "Oh, one of them," she said. Charlotte wasn't sure if she meant that being a pastor was one of them or the insurance company was one of them. She didn't say anything else.

"So, Reverend Charlotte Stewart, tell me what brings you into the office of a therapist."

Charlotte raised both eyebrows and gathered her hands in front of her. "Not sure exactly."

She waited. She had not expected to have to jump right into things. She had hoped or at least expected that there would be a little small talk at first. The direct hit of the counselor caught her off guard.

Marion did not ask anything else.

Charlotte decided to continue. "I was just beginning to feel . . ." She hesitated again, "I don't know." Another pause.

Marion kept waiting. She was motionless in her seat.

"I was just feeling, how do I say it?" Charlotte took in a breath. "I've been feeling lost." Then she sighed because she had said it.

"Lost." The counselor repeated like she was taking notes.

Charlotte thought that maybe the counselor was going to say something prophetic so she waited. But there was nothing more. She just sat high and confident in her seat without saying anything else. So Charlotte simply looked around the room. Marion just waited, letting her get acclimated to the office.

Charlotte noticed the pale peach walls and the Christmas cactus on a stand in the corner. She saw the big rubber ball up against the wall and quickly turned away, worried that rolling on a ball might be part of the first session. She observed the books on Marion's shelves, all about "living healed and healthy" and "a woman's right to love," and then she stopped at a picture that hung on the wall just behind the desk and chair. It was about two feet tall, an old brown frame with a stained and aging watercolor of a large black woman bending over a small plant.

"It's from a church book actually," Marion said when she noticed what Charlotte was studying. "It was in some section discussing the parable of Jesus about the seed planting. You know it?"

Charlotte nodded without facing the counselor.

"It's the one about the seed being sown in different places." She answered herself while she peered at the young pastor.

Charlotte was familiar with the text.

"I wonder which seed that one was." The therapist said this as she turned to study the picture.

Charlotte sat exploring the print, remembering the parable of Jesus.

"Well, I guess since it sprouted, it must have been the one that was planted in the good soil." Charlotte considered that she was wasting her time and money talking to this strange woman about a picture on a wall and a parable from the New Testament.

"Or maybe it was one of the seeds that was thrown along the path or on the rocky ground or even among the thorns, but the farmer found it and saved it, nurtured it with great tenderness and care, and it sprouted and grew after all." Marion said this and then focused on her client.

"It's a nice picture," Charlotte said with little thought as she continued to scan the room, impressed that the therapist knew the Bible story.

"Yep, my favorite," Marion replied.

There was a long and uncomfortable pause for Charlotte as she stared out the window watching some birds at a feeder. Marion didn't break the silence. She seemed perfectly at ease in the quiet. Finally Charlotte spoke again.

"I don't really know why I'm here," she confessed.

Marion did not respond.

"I just have been feeling," she struggled to find the right words, "empty or something." She leaned against the sofa. "I'm sort of isolated where I am and don't really have anyone to talk to. I thought it might be helpful to have a place to come and talk."

Marion smiled but still did not say anything.

Because of the lack of response, Charlotte kept on. "I pastor a little church out in the country. It's my first parish."

She observed Marion, who was only nodding. "We've had some tough things." She looked down in her lap and thought about Brittany and Nadine. She wondered if Nadine's conversations with psychologists or psychiatrists or whomever she spoke to went like this.

"One of my favorite people has cancer." And with that, a tear rolled from the corner of her eye.

Marion slid out of her seat with great effort and reached beside Charlotte to a box of tissues on the table and handed her one. Charlotte took it and wiped her face.

And she surprised herself at what came out of her mouth more than she surprised the therapist. "I'm not sure I believe there's a God anymore."

There was a moment of reflection. "Yeah," the older woman finally replied with ease, "it'd be nice if She made a grand announcement once in a while or sent us some miraculous sign just to let us know She's still up there." Marion struggled to get comfortable as she leaned into her chair.

Charlotte faced Marion and then inspected the older woman's hands. They were gnarled and bent, like those of someone who had suffered a stroke. The minister was amazed she had not noticed them before.

Marion noticed Charlotte's interest and held them out so they could be seen better.

"Arthritis, rheumatoid." She spread out her fingers. "That's why it's so much trouble for me to get around." She turned her hands over and back. "And that's why I'm so fat," she added with a smile.

"Best thing they got for the pain is steroids." She patted her stomach. "And God, do they make you hungry!" She laughed without a hint of regret or disappointment.

Charlotte suddenly realized that she was staring and quickly looked away.

There was another awkward pause.

"Tell me, Charlotte, how do you think of God?" Marion folded her hands back together and dropped them in her lap.

"You mean is he Father or Son or Holy Ghost?"

Marion shrugged, not answering.

"I don't know," she mumbled softly, unsure of how to reply.

Charlotte remembered her ideas from childhood of a *Leave It to Beaver* kind of father, a Santa Claus God, always interested in and providing for his children. That was what she had learned in Sunday School and from sermons and that was who she thought God was. However, since she had not had that kind of father herself, she was only able to connect that image of God to what she heard about, saw in those television Bible movies or in some of her friends' homes.

She remembered the pictures she had drawn of a big old man, wavy white hair and beard, long flowing robe, angels all around him, with room in his heart and on his lap for all the little children.

She remembered how later she had struggled with images of God when she studied the Old Testament, how she had not been comfortable with the notion that God was a warrior, telling his people to kill everyone in a town or village as they marched into the promised land, how he seemed violent and unforgiving in many of the stories. She remembered how she wrestled with the God in Job who let his righteous servant suffer so mercilessly at the hands of Satan, and how these images seemed so incompatible with the idea of God as loving shepherd or attentive father.

And what about history? She had questioned the Holocaust, lynchings, apartheid—where was the ever-present, ever-protective Father during those events?

Then she became a pastor and found herself involved in the personal struggles of people she cared about, people like Nadine and Louise, Lana and Wallace. And any image of God she tried to conjure up for herself or anyone else was never enough. She fought and struggled so long with trying to figure out God that she eventually tired of the battle and just gave up, deciding not to think about who God was, not to give herself a picture in her mind. This was the only way, she had decided, that she would be able then to do her work.

When she prayed, if she thought of anyone, envisioned anybody, she thought of Jesus, the tireless, patient rabbi who welcomed weary sinners and sided with the poor. She thought of his twisted broken body and his kind, gentle heart. And this mental picture, a picture of light in the darkness, had carried her through the long dry spells when she could not call up a face of God.

"God came to me once in a dream," Marion said, breaking the silence.

She realized by the expression on Charlotte's face that her client was not prepared or able to answer the question she had given her. So Marion was answering it herself.

"She was that woman, the farmer in the picture." She turned toward the picture.

"I resisted her at first."

Charlotte followed the counselor's eyes. The gardener in the picture had draped herself across the small fragile plant. She was holding up its leaves with both of her big, black hands, examining it, encouraging it to grow and bloom. The woman's face, like that of the angel in the garden, was dropped and hidden; and all that Charlotte could see was the top of an old straw hat and those caring, thick, worked, loving hands. She remembered her conversation with Nadine and the thoughts she had in the hospital about hands. She thought again about Marion's hands; but she did not turn to see them.

Marion dropped her chin and continued. "Some people think of her as the Black Madonna." She added, "You ever heard of her?"

Charlotte shook her head.

"It's funny but, apparently, lots of people have seen her. She mostly comes in times of trouble. She never talks," Marion said. "She just appears, just stands nearby, observing."

Marion shifted in her seat and crossed her ankles. "But everybody who has ever seen her is comforted by her presence. When I saw this picture, I knew it was her, the one who had visited me, in the dream." She pulled her elbows up and placed them on the arms of her chair. "That's why it's up there. And that's why it's my favorite."

"You think God's a big black woman?" Charlotte asked, not surprised, only interested.

"For now," Marion replied. "She comes to me in various disguises."

"So, you think that plant she's tending to is one of the seeds that wasn't supposed to make it, one of those sown in impossible circumstances." Charlotte was remembering the earlier part of their conversation about the parable Jesus told.

"I like the thought of that," Marion answered. The counselor waited a minute and then asked, "Do you garden?"

Charlotte lifted her shoulders and dropped them. "I was thinking about starting one this summer, but I never got around to it."

She remembered the dead flowers still in their pots behind the shed, how she had surveyed the property trying to find just the right spot to plant them.

"I garden," Marion said. "When I'm able." She gazed down at her twisted fingers and uncrossed her legs with some difficulty. Charlotte followed her eyes.

"It can be quite therapeutic," she added. She began bending and stretching her hands. "There's just something about getting in the dirt, watching the young seeds open and sprout, having the sun on your face, seeing things grow. It's a nice exercise in faith."

"Faith?" Charlotte asked, thinking it might be a nice exercise for the body or to rest the mind. But she wasn't sure how planting a garden had anything to do with one's faith. She thought of her recent sermon.

"Yep, faith." Then Marion explained. "You do all this stuff to get your garden ready, all this work. You break up the soil and add nutrients. You till and turn the dirt to get it rich and loamy. Then you go out and spend a lot of money on the finest plants or best seeds."

Marion's voice was soft and soothing, and Charlotte considered how it calmed her.

"You dig just the right size hole or drop the seeds exactly the right number of feet apart, then you add fertilizer and water evenly and frequently. You put everything in the ground and then you just have to wait."

Marion paused as she turned to notice the birds at the window.

"A goldfinch!" she said loudly. "I thought they had all left!" She seemed pleased.

Charlotte looked out the window but turned back to Marion and waited for the rest of the story.

Marion faced Charlotte and realized that her client was still listening.

"Oh, yes, the garden of faith. Where was I?" Her brow wrinkled and fell. "Oh, right!" she answered herself, "the waiting." She took a breath.

"You wait for a sign that what you have done has been right and that the seed was good and took hold. You wait for something to happen in the brown earth. You wait for results or product or reward and see nothing for days on end. And finally," Marion said, her words delivered slowly and resolved, "one day, you walk out and you see signs of new life. You see a small yellow-green hair pushing through the cold, hard dirt or you see the wilted young plant standing upright and tall or you notice a new bloom or a deeper color or something alive and growing where before there hadn't been anything; and that's when you finally begin to understand."

Charlotte didn't realize it, but she was sitting on the edge of the sofa, waiting for the answer, waiting to know what it is you finally begin to understand.

Marion enjoyed the interest of her newest client, and she let the anticipation grow a little more before she finished. She even yawned, covering her mouth with the back of her knotty hand.

Charlotte raised her shoulders in an impatient gesture. "Yes?" she asked.

Marion continued, "You finally understand that you really didn't have anything to do with what's growing in your garden after all." She went on.

"I mean, you did stick some things in the ground and you did make a place for them and you did water and fertilize a little; you may have kept a few weeds at bay. But," Marion added, "none of the growing or the springing to life or the change from seed to plant or plant to fruit had anything to do with you."

She swept her feet under her chair. "It is and has always been completely in the hands of Her." She motioned over to the picture that they had been discussing. She waited before going on.

"That's what faith is really all about anyway. It's about relying on something or somebody other than yourself. Recognizing that you don't have to have everything figured out or sorted through or understood. It's within us but also beyond us, and grace teaches us that we can find and claim all of what we need, when we need it."

Marion cast her focus directly on Charlotte. "And either you believe it or you don't." Then she softened. "And the great thing is, whether you do or don't—because sometimes you do and sometimes you don't—the garden grows just the same." She stopped for a moment. "The farmer is always at work."

Charlotte rested against the sofa and let the words and the wisdom bring to light the places in her heart that had been hidden. She did not force anything or even expect a change. But she suddenly began to imagine feeling something inside her. It was not big or dramatic. It merely felt like the possibility of a shift, a lift up against the dirt, a delicate but undeniable stretch of stem toward sunlight.

Charlotte closed her eyes. Nothing, she thought, would alter the consequences of her life or rub out those things that hindered her believing. Nothing could erase the years of disappointment or wipe away all the sorrow and the loss. Nothing could blast through the layers of old grief. But there, under the watchful attention of a large crooked woman, supervised by a farming God, a slim thread of somebody else's confidence was just enough to loosen the memories, slide aside the doubts, just enough, just a tiny bit that was enough so that a narrow, slight ray of sunshine came in. Charlotte breathed in deeply and slowly. And for the last ten minutes they had together on this occasion of their first visit, the young and tentative minister and her therapist waited quietly in a thin but certain light.

Hope Springs Community Garden Club Newsletter

BEA'S BOTANICAL BITS

Bottle or Tap: Quenching the Thirst

My husband, Dick, says I drink too much water. He says that if I wouldn't drink so much, we could drive to Winston-Salem in less than an hour. (I often have to stop for purposes of comfort.) But like all of us, I don't listen to my husband. And in fact, I'm confident that if they were placed side by side, my kidneys would be determined to be better looking, stronger, and healthier than his.

But that is not the purpose of this article, so let me get to gardening. Ladies, there is no excuse for harm or neglect coming to your plants because of water errors. You must be attentive to the weather and the needs of your garden friends. Don't let them die of thirst or drowning. Common sense, gardeners! Stick your fingers in the dirt and check the soil. Water your plants as needed.

"You can't do this to me!" Louise yelled while her friend held her hand down. Beatrice moved away.

Louise had just taken the kettle off the stove, and, upon hearing Margaret's news, without thinking, she leaned her right hand on the red-hot eye of the stove, burning two parallel and narrow curves across the inside of her hand. She then dropped the kettle, splattering the hot water on the floor, on the lower cabinets, and on the women's legs. When she finally got to the sink, she turned on the faucet and pulled out the spray attachment. Warm water came first, then finally cold water splashed and poured on them until Margaret was able to take the sprayer away from her friend, plug up the sink, and put Louise's burned hand down into the water.

Margaret let go of Louise's arm and stepped behind her. Louise pulled her hand out and examined the red, blistering paths that now ran across her palm. They were raised and perfectly spaced, like two exact worms inching from finger to thumb. Louise cradled the burned hand across her chest, stepping from one foot to the other.

Margaret was bending over wiping up the water with paper towels while Beatrice went to get a mop from the garage. When she returned she examined Louise's burns. "We might ought to take you to the hospital," she said.

"What for?" Louise asked. "To spend a thousand dollars to have some medical student wrap it in gauze?" She stuck her hand in the water and winced. "I don't think so."

Beatrice rolled her eyes and Margaret shook her head and got a few more paper towels. She wiped up the rest of the spillage and threw the towels away. She pulled out a chair at the dining room table and sat down. Beatrice finished mopping and took the wet mop out the door.

Louise stayed at the sink, her eyes focused on what was outside the window. She kept pulling her hand out of the water and then sticking it back in.

"When did you find out?" she asked as Beatrice was walking in the door.

"Last week," Margaret answered. "I had a biopsy." She fiddled with the napkin holder, the salt and pepper shakers. "My surgery is in a couple of days."

Louise didn't reply for a few minutes, but Margaret knew she was angry because she hadn't been told sooner. Margaret understood that, whether she had intended it or not, the feeling of betrayal was a consequence of the decision not to tell her friends. She waited for Louise's rant or some question from Beatrice and actually preferred either to this lack of communication.

Louise lifted her hand out and looked again at her palm. She knew it was a bad burn, probably second, maybe third degree, but she saw no use in going to the doctor about it. She remembered her plans for the week, and she considered how she would be able to finish her chores with her right hand now useless. But still she did not say anything to Margaret. She dipped her palm again into the cool water.

Beatrice sat down at the table next to Margaret. She began smoothing out the tablecloth with her hands.

"It's going to rain," Beatrice announced, trying to make conversation.

Margaret slid over in her chair so that she could see out the glass on the back door. Louise noticed the sky too.

The black clouds were tightening and a storm was definitely brewing.

"There was a tornado warning in Randolph County last night," Beatrice continued. Neither of the other women replied.

There was a long, quiet pause.

Margaret turned her face toward the kitchen to speak to Louise. "I'm sorry I didn't tell you before now."

Louise didn't answer.

Margaret continued, "I was so shocked I didn't know how to say it."

"You went alone to have the biopsy?" Beatrice asked with a sympathetic voice.

Margaret hated the question and was unsure how the women would take the answer. "Charlotte was with me."

Louise nodded slowly. She did not change the expression on her face. "Well, at least you weren't by yourself." She sounded distant.

"Yes," Beatrice replied. "How nice to be able to take your pastor with you." She said it politely, with just the right amount of sincerity.

"Yes," Margaret replied. Then she added, "I had not meant to tell her either. But I stopped by the church to see about Nadine and it just came out."

Louise didn't respond. She really didn't need an explanation, she thought. It was clear what had happened. Her friend had chosen not to tell her that she had gone through a major crisis. Louise had been excluded. Like Jessie making a decision to move, Margaret had not involved her. And the decisions of her friends not to tell left Louise facing feelings of betrayal that burned more deeply than her recent wounds. She could not think of anything more to say.

"I'm sorry, Lou." Margaret hoped Louise would face her, but she didn't. She just stayed at the sink without turning aside.

"Bea, I just didn't know how to tell anybody," Margaret said, now talking to her other friend.

Beatrice smiled and tapped her hand on Margaret's arm.

Louise thought about Roxie and remembered how George had been the one to tell her about the Alzheimer's. She wondered why she kept being uninformed. Why did her friends suddenly push her away in times of distress? she questioned herself. Was she not a good listener? Was she too brusque? too overbearing? Louise pulled her hand out of the sink, wrapped it in a dishtowel, and headed toward the bathroom. She walked by Margaret and Beatrice. "I'll be right back," she said calmly.

"Do you need any help?" Margaret asked as the injured woman disappeared into the hall.

Louise merely shook her head. Margaret turned in her seat and sighed. She never knew there were so many elements of a sickness. Not only does a person have to take care of herself but she also has to care for her friends.

"Just give her a little time," Beatrice said.

It appeared to Margaret that Beatrice wasn't upset, and she felt glad about that. She smiled at her. Then she sighed again and got up from her chair and walked to the bathroom, where Louise was trying to stretch gauze around her wounds using only one hand. Margaret pushed herself beside her and took the roll of thin white fabric and began wrapping it around Louise's hand.

"It was not a personal thing," she explained as she tightened the gauze around Louise's palm.

"It was personal for me," Louise answered.

Then there was a long pause as Margaret pulled the bandage down and around and over the burns and up and above her thumb.

"I didn't know how to say it," Margaret said. "I mean, I just couldn't form the words enough for myself, so I couldn't imagine how to say it out loud for somebody else." Margaret finished and took the scissors that were on top of the commode and cut the end of the gauze.

"I never thought of me as just somebody else," Louise said painfully. She reached in the medicine cabinet and pulled out the tape and handed it to Margaret.

"You know what I mean," Margaret replied as she cut small pieces of tape and placed them on the bandage. "I'm telling you now."

"Yes, yes you are," Louise replied, taking the tape and gauze and putting them into the cabinet. Then she walked toward the dining room.

"You want to try the tea again?" Beatrice was standing in the kitchen, filling up the kettle.

Margaret and Louise stood next to the table.

"Yes, that's fine," Margaret replied. "But I'd like for us to sit down and finish talking."

Louise shrugged her shoulders and sat down. Margaret moved behind her and pulled out the chair next to her while Beatrice put the kettle on the stove. She got out three cups and three teabags.

"I'm sorry I waited to tell you." She placed her arms on the table. "Honestly, Lou, I don't know how to be sick. I don't know how you tell somebody that you're going to take a test that may change everything for you. I don't know why one person chooses to keep things inside or why another picks up the phone right away and asks for help. This is new for me. I don't know how to do it." She paused. "I just don't know how to do it."

Louise lowered her gaze. "See, that's the thing," she said quietly. "I always thought in a friendship, that there shouldn't have to be a knowing how to do it."

She glanced back up at Margaret. "I mean, if you care about somebody, if you truly are a friend, shouldn't it just be in a natural order to hear bad news and then go to the ones you love?"

She reached for a napkin with her right hand and then, remembering her recent accident, dropped her arm in her lap. "I mean, why should there have to be a thought process? Why shouldn't it just be fundamental?"

Margaret shook her head. "I don't know." She leaned toward Louise. "Is there anything fundamental about cancer?" Then she sat back in her chair. "I guess there are stages that are documented and basic questions everyone has. But aren't there as many ways to handle bad news and backbreaking news and life-changing news as there are people in the world?"

She rested her elbow on the table. Then she thought a minute and added, "If I remember correctly, when Roxie died you didn't ask me about going to the cemetery and camping out. You were in a lot of pain and you just went. By yourself." She emphasized the last two words.

Beatrice spoke from the kitchen. "I heard that," she said. "You were some sight that night!"

Louise drew in a breath, recalling that awful night and how she had made a choice to be alone after the funeral. She hadn't sought out the counsel or advice of her friend. She had just stolen George's car and driven herself out to the grave. Her friends came to find her.

Louise laid both hands on the table. She faced Margaret. "You're right. I'm sorry. I'm being selfish."

She reached over to touch her friend's arm. She was still angry at Margaret, still angry at Jessie, and she was still angry that friendship wasn't always enough. She wanted the relationships she shared with these two women to guarantee honesty and intimacy and an undeniable sharing of the heart. But she realized there were no guarantees regarding friendship. She understood that there are times when even friends turn away from the women they love. "How are you doing?"

Margaret smiled slightly. "I don't know."

Margaret rested her head against the chair and closed her eyes. She thought about the last few days and the state of her mind, her spirit. She thought of how she had not slept a full night since receiving the first phone call, how she tossed and turned for hours in the darkness.

After a few minutes Beatrice brought in the tea in cups she had placed on a platter. "Hot tea," she said. Then she added, "Good for whatever ails you!"

Louise pulled out the chair for Beatrice using only her left hand.

"I never thought I'd be afraid to die," Margaret said without changing her position at the table. "I thought I was this strong, independent, faithful person who would face sickness or death like some army officer or something." She reached for her cup and blew across the top of the tea.

"I thought I'd prepared myself for everything and that I could handle any disease or ailment or crisis." She put down the cup.

"I'm not really ready," she said as she turned toward Louise, then over toward Beatrice.

Both women appeared concerned, then Louise nodded knowingly.

Beatrice spoke up. "Yes, I always thought I had managed to be ready for everything too." She relaxed in her chair.

"Did I ever tell you how I imagined everyone dying so I'd be primed for the pain?" Louise stretched for her cup; she seemed better.

Margaret and Beatrice waited for the story.

"That's what I used to do on the weekends." She set the cup down, pulled her chair closer to the table, and then started to take a sip.

Margaret shook her head as she took a swallow. "You mean to tell me your leisure time was spent killing off people in your mind?" She wondered if this was why Louise always seemed so prepared for the deaths of her family members, how she managed to be so strong and put together.

"Yep," Louise said without appearing embarrassed. "Got everybody too. Mama, Calvin, Bitsy, Aunt Myrtle. I saw them all slain before it happened." She leaned forward. "And for the most part I was plenty ready." She paused a second.

"And then . . ." Louise put down her cup and dropped her arms at her side. "I loved Roxie."

Margaret closed her eyes again and listened while Beatrice watched her friend.

"And as hard as I tried, even after she married George and I thought I'd lost her, I could not think of her dying." Louise sat up and started again to drink her tea but then kept talking.

"Even when she moved in here and I was supposed to know about her forthcoming death and be prepared." She slid down in her seat. "There's some things your heart simply refuses to acknowledge." She hesitated. "There are ideas and notions that just cannot be considered."

Margaret remembered Roxie's funeral and afterward how Louise had grieved. She recalled how difficult the year had been for her friend and thought that maybe her reasons for not telling her about the mammogram and biopsy had been a fundamental response after all. Maybe her choice was meant not to cause Louise any more pain. And with that idea, she wondered if she should say anything in this regard but then decided just to keep silent.

"I guess there's really no way to be prepared for life's little surprises," Beatrice said.

"No," Louise responded, "I guess not."

"And," Louise added, "I guess there's no real way to know what you'll need from your friends when you run into those little surprises either."

Margaret shook her head. Louise glanced out the window and noticed how dark the sky was turning. "I think that storm is about to break," she said as she drank from her cup. Then she spat out her drink and yelled, "This tea tastes like shit, Beatrice." She put down the mug. "Where did you get this?"

Beatrice took a sip. She swallowed and then acted confused. "It's something you had up in your cabinet."

Louise thought for a moment. "What kind of box was it in?" she asked.

"Yellow, I think," Beatrice answered. "With lots of writing on the box." She put down her cup. "I didn't have my glasses so I couldn't read it."

"Beatrice, this is a laxative tea. I bought it for Roxie." She sat back in her chair. "It's called Easy Movement and it tastes like what it's supposed to make happen."

Margaret laughed and Beatrice drank some more and then licked her lips. "Well, I think it's fine."

Louise got up from the table and took some water from the refrigerator. She poured a glass for herself and one for Margaret, who was apparently not too thrilled with the tea either.

"You know, I never liked my titties," Beatrice said as Louise was sitting down.

Margaret took her glass from Louise and listened in disbelief to Beatrice.

"They were always too big, bouncing all around all the time." She put her hands under her breasts.

"And my shoulders have actual dents in them from wearing chest girdles all my life!" She rubbed her left shoulder with her right hand. "Have you all ever seen my breasts?"

Margaret shook her head while Beatrice started to unbutton her blouse.

Louise quickly responded. "Beatrice, if you flop those things out on my dining room table, I swear I'm calling the police."

"Oh all right, Ms. Prude." She pulled her blouse together. "Well, anyway, I almost considered having them taken off!"

Margaret was still stunned.

"You mean a size reduction," Louise said in a sort of callous way.

"No, I mean cut off," Beatrice answered. "What did I need these things for anymore? I had already nursed all the babies I was ever going to nurse. And I didn't really foresee a future in exotic dancing." She took another sip. Louise grimaced at the thought of Beatrice dancing naked.

"Well," Margaret asked, "what happened?" She was curious.

"Dr. Lucas said he wouldn't do it." Beatrice dropped her face, her chin resting on her chest. "He said I should be grateful for what I had and that my husband was a lucky man."

Louise was shocked. "He said that to you?"

"Yes, he did."

"What did you say?" Margaret asked in astonishment.

"I said that Paul Newgarden wasn't a breast man and that even if he was, his luck did not have anything to do with the size of his wife's boobs but everything to do with the fact that I was a good woman and that he was fortunate to be married to me." She said this loudly and with a lot of pride as she remembered that doctor visit from many years ago.

"Huh," Margaret said in reply. "I can't say as I've ever had such a conversation with my doctor."

"Well," Beatrice responded, "that's because you have normal breasts."

Margaret glanced over at Louise and started to laugh.

"What?" Beatrice asked innocently.

"What does having normal breasts have to do with having that kind of conversation with a doctor?" Margaret took a drink of her water.

"It has everything to do with that."

Louise and Margaret waited for the explanation.

"If you have normal breasts, then you wouldn't have asked for them to be taken off. And if you were not to ask to have them taken off, then you would not have heard your doctor say such a thing." Beatrice said it so reasonably that Margaret and Louise thought they must have missed some step in the process since they still did not understand.

"Never mind, Beatrice," Louise said. "What kind of surgery are they doing?" she asked Margaret.

Margaret was still thinking about Beatrice's story as she answered Louise's question. "They're going ahead to do a mastectomy." She paused, then explained. "They were going to do a lumpectomy; but they're concerned that isn't enough, that based on the test results, it would be better to go ahead and take the whole breast. That way, if it's . . ." She stopped. "If the cancer's spread, they wouldn't have to go back and do another operation."

There was silence at the table as the three women considered what was about to take place. They watched the sky and thought of storms and loss and the sorrow inherent in the surgery Margaret was facing. They listened to the approaching thunder and the whirling of wind and sat with their sadness, wondering how much of what they felt should be shared.

"You know, I said I wanted them off at one time, but truthfully," Beatrice's voice was calm, "I would miss mine if they were gone."

She placed her hand across her chest as if she was pledging allegiance to something.

Louise tried to reach under the table to pinch Beatrice, but she was sitting too far away. She thought this sort of talk was bad for Margaret. But then she turned toward her friend and noticed that Margaret appeared not to be put off or uncomfortable with Beatrice's ideas.

"What do you mean, Bea?" Margaret asked.

"I don't know," she replied as the storm picked up outside. Then she added, "They are a part of what makes us women."

Louise wanted to put an end to the topic. "Let's get out of here and get some lunch before this weather breaks." She stood up from her seat.

"No," Margaret responded, "I want to talk about this."

And Louise sat down, glaring at Beatrice, who did not notice.

"Do you think they really make us women?" Margaret asked.

Beatrice reached up and cupped her breasts. Louise watched her, then faced Margaret, who was staring at her own chest.

"Breasts do not make us women," Louise said, almost in anger.

"Then what does?" Margaret asked. "Is it our wombs or our vaginas?"

Beatrice pulled her knees toward her chest and started rolling up her dress.

"Beatrice Newgarden Witherspoon, don't even think about it!"

Beatrice dropped the hem of her dress and drank some more tea. It annoyed her that Louise could be so modest.

"I don't know, Margaret," Beatrice said as she sighed at Louise and then spoke to her other friend. "I guess I've always thought it was a physical thing. That the definition of our gender did have to do with what is or isn't a part of our bodies." Then she added, "Male, penis, female, no penis."

Margaret replied, "Well, now you're saying that being a woman has to do with not having the male organ. That we're female because, by process of being denied a penis, we're not male."

Beatrice reflected on this notion. "Yes, I guess I am." She hesitated. "But then what about the titties?"

"What about the titties?" Margaret asked.

"Could you maybe use a different word than titties?" Louise asked. "It sounds so . . . locker room, or something." She was still trying without much success to put a halt to the talk that was taking place at her dining room table.

"Being a woman is about not having a penis; and it is about having . . ." Beatrice hesitated then said with a certain amount of dignity, "breasts." She turned to Louise, who smiled a fake smile.

"Which then brings us back to my situation," Margaret responded.

Beatrice's brow was knotted in concentration.

"If I lose my breasts, then am I no longer a woman?"

"Of course not," Louise exclaimed in disbelief at the entire conversation.

"Hold on!" Beatrice replied. "It's a good question. And I need to think about that."

The three women sat in silence for a few minutes, two of them considering what it means to be a woman, one of them trying to figure out how to change the subject.

"Okay, let's look at this," Beatrice said like she was a scientist.

Louise started to her feet and Margaret spoke up. "Oh, I don't think she means look in a literal way, Lou!" Margaret said, and the other woman sat back down. "You don't, do you, Bea?"

Beatrice shook her head and continued. "If a baby is born female, there are certain body parts it has and certain body parts it does not have. And when the doctor sees which parts there are, the doctor decides if it's a boy baby or a girl baby." Beatrice nodded as if she had come up with the right answer.

"But what if the baby has both parts, or some of one and some of another?" Margaret had heard of such births from her niece who was a labor and delivery nurse.

Louise exhaled loudly. This line of thinking was just too much for her. She began to notice a throbbing in her hand, and she took another sip from her glass of water.

"Then it's genetic," Beatrice answered. "It's the XY chromosome thing. Whether you're male or female has to do with your NBA strand."

Louise almost spit up her drink. "NBA? NBA? Is that what you said?"

Margaret started to laugh. "Oh my God, that's what she said!"

Beatrice quickly realized her mistake. "DNA, I meant to say. DNA!" She kicked Louise's leg. "It isn't very nice to make fun of others."

"You're right." Louise stopped, sounding almost apologetic. Then she added, "But sometimes it just bounces out of me!" And she laughed some more.

Margaret covered her mouth, trying not to laugh, but it was funny to her. And to hear Louise and Beatrice now fighting about it made it even funnier.

"You are not my friend!" Beatrice got up from the table as if she was wounded.

"Oh, come back, Bea," Margaret called after her.

"Bea, come here!" Louise hollered into the kitchen. "I was only kidding."

"You're not that funny, you know," Beatrice said as she walked to the table. She had gotten a banana from the fruit bowl.

"I know. And my hook shot is a little off, too." Louise punched Beatrice in the arm. "Must be because I don't have a penis."

Margaret shook her head. "Bea, I know what you meant."

"Thank you, Margaret."

"And I really have thought about what it means to lose a breast. I have thought that it will make me less a woman." She slumped a bit in her chair.

Louise folded her arms about her chest. "It's just not so, Margaret. Being a woman isn't about body parts. It isn't just about science and genes and penises." She leaned away from the table. Her voice was strong and steady. And she finally sounded ready to confront her friends.

"Then what's it about, O wise one?" Beatrice asked as she peeled her banana, waiting to be enlightened.

"Okay, I don't know. Or maybe I do know." She hesitated. "Of course, it's about what's on the outside, our physical makeup. It does have to do with breasts and wombs and not having a penis. I don't deny that."

Beatrice nodded knowingly.

Louise continued. "But it's also about giving birth and having periods and . . ." She paused. "It's also about the nature of our hearts."

Margaret and Beatrice were surprised to be hearing this from Louise.

She fidgeted with the bandage on her hand, trying to think of the right words she wanted to say. She mumbled at first and then spoke loud enough for the other women to understand her. "I think we have a greater capacity to love than men," she said.

"What?" Beatrice asked. She was confused by what her friend was saying.

Louise shifted, placing both hands on the table. "I think women make better friends. I think we know more about love."

Margaret sat up in her seat and considered this line of thinking. "Do you really think that, Lou?" She wanted to believe it. "I mean, do you really, actually think that?"

The mood changed, and the women became quiet.

Louise seemed a bit embarrassed that she had suddenly become so vulnerable. She simply nodded her head.

"Well, I think it's a lovely thought," replied Beatrice as she continued to eat the banana. "And frankly, even though I hate to admit it"—she picked up a napkin and pulled it along the edges of her lips—"I think she's right." She wrapped the peeling in the napkin.

"Well, it ain't basketball!" Louise said jokingly. "But I just can't believe that being a woman is only a physical arrangement. There's got to be more to it than that."

Margaret seemed satisfied that what her friend had said was true. It comforted her, pleased her, and she was glad to have spoken her fears out loud.

Louise held up her half-full glass. "Being a woman is like water," she said, as the other women waited for her to finish.

"You can freeze it, boil it, drink it, spill it, leave it in the sun and evaporate it; but it will still be water. And being a woman is the same." Louise took note of her wounded hand. "You can remove her body parts, take away her children, her capacity to bear children, bind her, break her, dismiss her; but it will not stop who she is." And this she said with the greatest confidence, "We will always be women."

Margaret smiled. And just at that moment, while three friends sat together and measured their womanness, the sky opened up and the rain fell hard.

Hope Springs Community Garden Club Newsletter

BEA'S BOTANICAL BITS

Knowing Your Parts

"Parts is parts," I was told once by an old salesman. "Gotta have 'em working whether you're talking about a long-legged tap dancer or a lawn mower." Everything counts.

Plants, like us women, are made up of several parts. These parts include the root, the stem, and the leaves.

Now as I have mentioned in previous articles, soil, water, and light are all important to the health and condition of the plant. But the truth is, the plant itself holds the secret to its life. It's got to be strong, with its parts in good condition, in order to survive and flourish. You can wine and dine and shine it, but if the parts of the plant aren't stacked up and putting forth effort, you might as well yank it by the roots and bury it. That sucker's already dead.

When Nadine confessed that the accident had been an attempt at suicide, her third, the doctor stepped away from the bed as if she were contagious and made a note on her chart that sent nurses and social workers and the chaplain in and out of her room with faces of worry and faraway gazes that seemed to Nadine to be made up of genuine sorriness.

"We're transferring you somewhere you can get better care," he had said. And she was moved to the psychiatric unit as soon as she was able to get up and walk to the bathroom.

She was placed in a private room on the sixth floor that was sparse of furniture and color but never devoid of light. During the day the overhead tubular bulb could not be turned off, and at night a large and bright lamp burned outside the window, which was covered with iron bars but had no curtain or blinds.

"Darkness frightens many of our patients," a therapist had replied unapologetically when she asked about the constant light.

And even with the glaring brightness outside and above her, members of the hospital staff often came to her bedside to shine a flashlight in her eyes.

"Are you doing this to see if I'm asleep or dead?" she asked, but never received an answer. And after five weeks in the behavior modification ward, Nadine became accustomed to the light and the hourly checks, learning how to sleep in fifty-minute increments.

She attended all the groups, had individual sessions with a psychiatrist and a therapist, and watched television in the dayroom with the other patients, who were not always coherent or polite. She learned stories of violence and deaths that kept her dreams grave and horrific. She eased into the program without a lot of difficulty; but she often felt frightened at the amount of pain she encountered both within herself and outside in others.

In the thirty-five days of treatment she saw teenagers lost to anger and disillusionment, old people crazed and forgotten, and many, like herself, somewhere between youth and maturity, caught in an event or circumstance that seemed to overshadow everything else.

She heard countless stories of suicide ventures, too many accounts of rape and abuse, numerous ways to get high, and repeated patterns, like her own, from those who did not know how to move forward in the lives they had been given. Those she met lived hard and brutal lives. They were rough and spindly souls with very shallow roots.

In her stay at the special ward, she signed in only two visitors, her mother and Charlotte. When Nadine heard that Ray had given his mother-in-law the message that he would like to come and see her, she offered no reply and merely lowered her eyes away from her mother's face and turned to watch *Who Wants to Be a Millionaire,* which was blaring from across the room.

It wasn't that she was mad at Ray or regretted that their relationship had ended. It was just that he was so physically altered by the death of their daughter, so broken by it, that she could not stand to find her face in the eyes of someone who suffered too close to the surface. It was like staring into the mouth of hell, tortured souls and grasping hands calling her down and away from any remote possibility that she had manufactured for herself that she would be okay.

She figured that Ray would like her to die, for both of them to die, but that he did not have the stomach to kill either of them, and he would simply rather live his life pushing and pulling himself through a ragged grief that cut and maimed him, a kind of slow and agonizing death that Nadine couldn't choose.

The last time she had seen him he tore at his temples until they bled, and when she had given him the gun to shoot her and then himself, he only dropped his face in his hands, a sign, in her mind, of his cowardice. She left him then and decided that if she was going to die, she would have to do it for herself, and if she was going to live, she would have to find some way other than the diminished one he had chosen for himself.

Nadine told the doctor about her daughter's death and her divorce. She told the counselor about the drug use and what she had done on the three occasions of her attempts at suicide. She told her grief group and her substance abuse group that she didn't remember anything about Brittany's funeral but that everyone said it was lovely, and that she did not always enjoy how it felt to be drunk or high but that she preferred it to how she felt when she was sober.

It seemed to everyone assigned to Nadine Klenner's case that she was open and honest and making relative advancement toward a more healthy means of coping with the loss of her child. She was given red checks beside her name and had moved up from step 1 to step 4, which meant she was working the hospital program and could receive more benefits. Step 5 was the highest you could go before you were discharged. And although the nurse and social worker agreed that she was ready, Nadine wasn't sure she wanted to have her own television in her room or be released to other parts of the hospital like the solarium and the cafeteria. She wasn't sure she liked the idea of getting closer to being discharged and having to try it again on her own. She wasn't sure she was ready for the real world or the paralyzing grief that waited for her at home. She wasn't sure she ever wanted to leave the hospital and face again the shock of darkness.

Besides, she was satisfied with step 4, where she stayed confined to the unit, eating in the small dining room with plastic utensils and very little flavoring and watching TV with the rest of the patients. She was comfortable with the rules and predictability of the staff and their suicide checks. She was at ease with the daily schedules and the locked doors and the lack of visitors. She was completely relaxed with how things were done for the patients who had not graduated to the final level. And so, this is where she stayed right up until her last two weeks.

Other than Nadine herself, only Charlotte knew what the others did not. Nadine was not, as the nurses reported in their meetings, "well and recovering."

She was not, as her therapist had said, "beginning to function in a normal capacity."

She had merely learned the meaning of the title "compliant patient" and was acting it out, and it was working for everyone except her.

She knew that the staff would not see it because they were invested in her success: they needed her to get better, they needed the bed for the next mental patient. The doctor hadn't noticed because he was busy trying to fill out paperwork and decide which insurance companies to align himself with. Her mother would not acknowledge it because she had no room left in her heart for disappointment. Only Nadine and Charlotte saw and knew it for what it was. Nadine identified it because it was her own shrunken soul. And Charlotte understood because she was clearly proficient in recognizing the fake appearance of good faith.

Nadine wrestled with her demons between the bed checks, after the beam of light shone in her eyes and before the next knock on the door. She tried to pray, without success, and asked for God to kill her himself, so that she might at least be saved from that curse and judgment. She pleaded for death in the lighted darkness, and only when the sun rose did she wipe the tears from her eyes, repeat the mantras of healthy grief that everyone wanted to hear, and pretend that she was heading up and away from her sadness.

Charlotte saw it right away, during the first visit, and couldn't decide how it might best be said and whether she should say it to a staff member or just save it for Nadine. She wasn't sure how to broach the subject with anyone. She was uncomfortable in the setting anyway. So she did not know whether she would be able to talk coherently about what she had observed with anybody who worked there.

The minister visited Nadine on Thursdays, since most of her office work was completed by then and her sermon was done. It did not interfere with Bible Study or the afternoon youth program. There were no regularly scheduled committee meetings in the evening, so she had time to unwind when she returned.

She was uncomfortable when she went to the psychiatric unit because she did not like the ward and its prisonlike accommodations. When she visited Nadine she had to leave her purse with the charge nurse, sign in at two separate desks after displaying her photo identification, and walk through three secured doors that buzzed when a staff member read her paperwork and decided she was allowed to enter.

The entire process to visit her parishioner was unnerving, and usually Charlotte asked to talk with Nadine in her hospital room rather than in the dayroom, because the other conversations and the television noise just seemed more than she could stand. Nadine didn't care one way or the other and would lead her pastor down the hall and into her room, slumped and slow.

This particular week Charlotte came early because Margaret was going in for her surgery the following day, and the Cookbook Committee was planning a special dinner in her honor. Charlotte wanted to get home in time.

It was rainy and windy, an unseasonably cold day for the mild climate of North Carolina, and Charlotte had not dressed appropriately. The weather had changed quickly and the pastor had not prepared herself for the sudden chill. She shivered, sliding her hands up and down her arms as she followed Nadine to her room.

"Cold outside?" the patient asked.

"Yep. Wet, you know, like it was already Halloween or November."

Nadine pushed open the door to her room and they both walked in.

"Here, use this blanket," Nadine said as she yanked the cover off the bed and threw it to Charlotte.

Charlotte took it and wrapped it around herself while Nadine jumped on the bed and leaned against the wall behind her. Charlotte pulled the chair away from the desk and turned it toward Nadine; then she sat in it.

"You're not cold?" she asked as she gathered the blanket around her.

Nadine shook her head and peered beyond Charlotte out the door at another patient walking by.

"Grandma, say a prayer for me."

The old woman made a huffing noise and then replied, "You ought to pray your own self and you ought to quit smoking. Goin' kill you and it makes your hair stink." She shuffled past the room.

"That's Grandma. She thinks she's at a church." Nadine spoke quietly. "And she's got a thing about everybody smoking."

Charlotte turned and watched as the old woman moved away from the door. She was small, wiry, and sharp; and she pushed her walker in front of her, paused, then pushed on toward the end of the hall. She was humming a song that Charlotte remembered from her early days in church, an old spiritual, "Swing Low" or maybe "Jacob's Ladder." Charlotte wasn't sure. She turned to face Nadine.

"So, what's this week been like?" Her tone was light, friendly. It was her third time in the hospital room; and it was as she remembered and as Nadine's mother had reported, dismal and empty. The pastor didn't understand why they couldn't at least paint the walls a more cheerful color or put a wallpaper border around the top. It seemed so sterile and unfeeling, so devoid of any possibility of healing.

"Well, we still haven't done any leather crafts, if that's what you're asking." Nadine began to pick at her nails.

Charlotte teased, "Shoot, I was sort of hoping for a new wallet."

Nadine smiled. She liked Charlotte, always had. "I'm doing okay," she responded as if somebody else had asked, and Charlotte again recognized the untruth.

"I forgot to ask you last time about what happened when you told your doctor. Your mom said he sort of freaked." Charlotte stretched her legs out in front of her. She tried to get comfortable. "What was that about?"

Nadine shrugged. "He was out the door before he even finished examining me. I swear you'd have thought I yelled out the word *malpractice!*" She shook her head.

"But it's all right. I knew this is where I needed to be anyway." She pulled one of her legs across the other.

"It took a lot of courage to tell him, Nadine." Charlotte met her eyes. Then Nadine turned away.

"You know, I think you'd like my psychiatrist." Nadine changed the subject, and Charlotte could tell she was only trying to keep the conversation at a particularly superficial depth.

"Yeah?" Charlotte asked, playing along.

"Yeah, he's cute, wears clogs." Nadine lifted her chin and tried to sound interested. "Single too, I think."

"Yeah? What makes you think that?" Charlotte was curious about this assessment.

Nadine slid her right hand over her left fourth finger. "No ring," she answered.

"Well, that doesn't mean he's not married," Charlotte responded.

"Yep, but he flirts a lot with the nurses," Nadine replied.

"Well, that certainly doesn't tell us for sure if he's single." Charlotte tucked the blanket under her legs. "Married people do flirt, I hear."

"Has a married man ever flirted with you?" Nadine asked innocently.

Charlotte narrowed her eyes. "I wasn't speaking from personal experience."

Nadine blurted out the next question quickly. "When's the last time you went on a date?" She knew lots of people in the church had wondered, but she figured no one had ever asked the pastor.

"Lord, Nadine, I don't know." Charlotte considered the question. "I guess a couple of years ago. I went to a wedding with another preacher. We drove together and had dinner afterward, so I guess that would count as a date."

"You like him?" Nadine threw her arms behind her head and waited for the response. She liked being able to ask the questions.

"Not really," Charlotte answered. "Preachers, I don't know. I don't think I'd want to be with a preacher."

"Why not?" Nadine asked.

Charlotte remembered the men in seminary, how they paraded their faith in front of everybody with bravado, how they struggled earnestly with the plight of the poor and their own privileged situations of studying poverty in a classroom. She thought of how they talked about God and their relationships with him like they were old friends from high school or equals, how they secretly relished the notion that they had been set apart and called to lives that they believed distinguished them from other men, but how they liked to appear as if they really fought with their decisions to commit. She remembered how they swaggered effortlessly from class to class, trying to appear burdened and pensive but all the time concerned that nobody else was watching.

"Why are you suddenly so interested in my love life?" Charlotte was uncomfortable with the discussion and was not pleased with her refreshed memories.

There was a pause as another patient walked down the hall and stopped at the door. He didn't speak, just stuck his head in, then moved to the room next door. Nadine shrugged her shoulders.

There was an awkward pause.

"We talk a lot in here." Nadine got up and shut the door, then returned to the bed. "Everybody says what they feel about things."

Charlotte remembered her visits with Marion and wondered again if the conversations were anything like the ones she was having.

"And there's always a group meeting." She hesitated as she recalled the lengthy sessions where everything was open for discussion, the raw and uncensored way the patients talked. She added with a certain amount of pride, "It seems like everybody thinks I'm doing good."

Charlotte thought that Nadine sounded like she was trying to convince herself.

"What do you think?" Charlotte was easy with her question.

"I don't know." She shook her head. "I don't know what to think."

Charlotte understood perfectly. There were some things that could not be measured or analyzed. Some moods that couldn't be described in thinking terms. Sometimes it was good just to have gotten through the day without crying or throwing yourself out the window. But that still doesn't mean that you can explain how you think about it.

A bell rang that reminded Charlotte of changing classes in school. Charlotte waited for Nadine to explain it.

"That's for another group. Exercise class for the kids."

Charlotte nodded. There was a long pause.

"I blame myself for this, you know. I figure everybody else does too."

Charlotte wasn't sure what she meant, and Nadine knew she would have to elaborate.

"I was negligent with Brit. I shouldn't have made you baby-sit her all those times."

A woman screamed and there was a rush of staffers in the hall. The conversation stopped for a few minutes until the tussle was over. Charlotte got up to see what was happening but then moved back to where she had been sitting. She wondered if Nadine was finished.

Nadine went on. "And I didn't have her in the backseat with her seat belt on. She was still supposed to be in the backseat." Nadine took a breath and explained. "They make these car seats for children her age and I hadn't bought one because I thought she was big enough to sit up front."

Charlotte closed her eyes and hoped that Nadine wouldn't say anything more. But the young woman, locked up and defenseless, had one more thing to say. The final piercing truth that she had never spoken out loud to anyone.

"I killed my baby. And I don't know what to do about it."

There, she thought, I said it. And it was easier than she had imagined. She changed her position, pulled her legs under her, but she didn't cry or cover her face. She just stayed as she was, her body relaxed and at rest, a young woman lounging on a bed.

Charlotte didn't speak. She simply sat back, remembering how she had walked up on a conversation at the grocery store not too long after the wreck. Two young women about her age had pushed their carts off to the side and were discussing the accident as if they had discovered its cause and justification. They acted as if they could explain it away, as if they had drawn it up and figured out the reasons for such tragedy, cleaned it up and given it a name so that they could hold it far and away from themselves. Charlotte had listened as they spoke in hushed and persuasive tones.

"Nadine did not take care of her little girl. Why, I remember when Brit was a baby, she didn't hold it right. She let the head dangle off to the side. Mama said she wasn't able to care for that child."

One of the women was thin, tight-lipped, and nervous. She was dressed like she was on her way to do aerobics or run or have a game of tennis. She shifted from side to side as she spoke. Her face was red, glowing with the news.

The other one was broad-faced and animated. She joined in. "I know it. I saw her one time with that baby in the middle of February and that child did not have anything on its arms."

This woman reached over to the shelf behind her and grabbed two bags of barbecue potato chips without taking a breath. "And what was she doing coming out that way from the church parking lot? Everybody knows you can't see anything from that end of the driveway." She threw the bags in her cart.

Charlotte had stood across from them, not knowing whether she should speak. She knew they were unfairly judging Nadine, but she also realized that they were merely trying to convince themselves that they wouldn't drive a car into the path of another or that they were not so careless as to allow death to snatch up their own babies. She knew that in the face of suffering, people, especially mothers, came up with anything they could think of to keep their own fears at bay.

They became rash and ugly just so they would not have to lie awake at night and actually face the terror that had wrapped around their babies and slid out with them when they were born. Charlotte knew that once a mother's womb tightened and cramped, once she widened herself to make room for the delivery, once she arched her back and pushed the life from inside herself, she knew that she had also given birth to panic. A panic so stark and looming that if she gave in to it, let herself think about it, toyed with the possibilities of it, she would gather up her babies and push them back inside herself. The idea that her child could die is simply more than any mother can stand.

Charlotte had not confronted them. She did not speak to their injustice or their loose tongues. She did not ram her shopping cart into theirs or pass them a cold stare that they would surely not miss. She did not wave her finger in their faces and accuse them of arrogant meanness or idle gossip. She simply walked by them with her head down. She was so devastated from the death herself that she did not have the strength to yell into somebody else's grief.

But now, surprisingly, she did. She sat up a little so she could see into Nadine's eyes.

"Nadine, I don't know why Brittany died. I have sought hundreds, no, thousands of times to try to lay it out, fold it up, and stick it in a drawer somewhere so that when I was ready I could pull it out and deal with it."

Charlotte lifted the blanket up to her chin. "I helped her into the front seat." She paused. "I didn't pull the seat belt around her."

Nadine studied the young pastor as she claimed her own responsibility in the suffering.

"I was the last one with her, the last one to touch her. I could've kept it from happening." Charlotte dropped her eyes. "It's as much my fault as it was yours."

Nadine didn't move from the bed. She thought maybe she should climb over to Charlotte, that maybe they should hug or touch or something; but she just couldn't push herself that far. So they just stayed like that, locked in the pain of being involved in evil and incapable of stepping beyond it.

Nadine finally shook her head and spoke. "I don't blame you. I never blamed you."

Charlotte replied quickly, "And I don't blame you."

Nadine turned away. "Yeah, but I blame me. And until I stop blaming me, I can't figure out what reason I got to get through the day."

Charlotte had nothing. She thought about how she had felt for years after Serena died, how she anguished over it, felt responsible for it. Even now, she wondered how it could have been different. She thought how Serena might have been helped in a place like where Nadine was, or how she would have lived if Charlotte had made the decision to see her that weekend, how a moment could have changed everything.

But she also knew that an obsession like believing you are responsible for the death of somebody else can spread like a virus until everything inside a heart and a soul and mind is infected and destroyed. She knew all too well that taking that belief into yourself is like swallowing a fuse and then sitting back and waiting until every organ in your body is blown up and nothing is left but a shell, the insides scrambled like a bomb has gone off.

She knew there was nothing quick and easy about redemption. She understood it wasn't always available at the moment or in the package and the size one felt was needed. It wasn't always a sweet walk with Jesus in some garden near an empty but lily-laden grave.

And that sometimes there wasn't anything anybody could bring down from some altar or out from the pages of a book or even pulled from the beating heart of a God who allowed for the killing of his own son, that could ease away the constant clamor of guilt.

She knew that taking in mercy is like waiting on dawn in the middle of the night. A person just has to know it's coming, just has to accept that it's the one undying promise, just has to believe it without understanding it or pretending that she will evolve into someone who deserves it. A person just has to lie down and go to sleep expecting the morning to come. And that decision, that willingness to put down the doubts and the excuses and the blame and sorrow, that can only be made by the one hurting. Even God can't do that. Charlotte realized that everybody, at some time in her life, has to decide about her own survival. And no one can be completely sure of what she'll choose when the time comes.

And Charlotte understood that Nadine was going to have to make up her own mind about forgiveness, about survival. And as she sat in the psychiatric hospital, facing the stark walls, the hard, unyielding corners of the room, and the crude, exposed pain of somebody else, she understood that she would have to make up her mind about herself as well. It was as Marion had said, either she would believe or she would not. Only she could decide that. No matter how much the farmer stays working the fields, the plant ultimately decides its own fate. Everybody chooses to keep breathing.

"You don't know what Brittany and I talked about the day she died, do you?" Charlotte got up from her chair and walked over to the barred window. She saw traffic spilling out of the parking lot, the road heavy with employees changing shifts and visitors coming in.

Nadine placed her elbows on her knees. Charlotte had won her interest.

"She wanted to know about heaven and about my sister, who died a few years ago."

Nadine leaned her forehead into the soft place on the inside of her arm. She had not considered the conversation the preacher had with her daughter that day. She had not thought it was important.

"She wanted to know if people were happy in heaven and if they would be able to return to earth. . . ." Charlotte stared straight ahead, out into the cloudy sky, the spirited autumn wind, remembering the conversation. She continued, "To visit the people they loved."

Nadine didn't speak. There was an announcement over the loudspeaker about an art group meeting in the assembly room. Neither woman seemed to hear it.

Charlotte stood away from the bed. The blanket draped around her like a cape. "It's weird, but it's like she knew or something."

Nadine started to shake her head, then stopped.

"And she wasn't nervous or upset or concerned."

Charlotte remembered the morning. She remembered how odd she thought the topic of the conversation was when the little girl began it, how she, the pastor, felt uncomfortable with the questions, the idea of considering and discussing the afterlife. She remembered how Brittany played with the toys on the shelf, without thought or trouble, how she asked about Serena and whether there would be animals in heaven.

Charlotte added, "She said that she would come back and tell me about my sister."

The minister pulled the blanket around her at the waist. She did

not look over to the dead girl's mother. She stayed as she was, waiting at the window, watching the people hurry in and out, the wind tossing them about. "I've never told anyone this because I don't know what I think about it. But, Nadine, I wonder, maybe she knew."

Charlotte hesitated, then turned around to face Nadine, her body wrapped inside the hospital spread. "Do you think I'm crazy for telling you this?"

Nadine didn't change. She didn't agree or tell her to stop or shift the focus of her gaze.

Charlotte kept on. "You know, she wasn't mad."

The pastor moved so that she was able to see the young woman eye to eye. It was the truest thing she had ever said. "She doesn't blame you."

Nadine did not look at the preacher. She did not respond out loud. She simply heard the questions as they pounded in her brain. How does a child know she's going to die? How can a little girl be ready to die, be at peace with leaving everything she knows? How could a baby understand what it means to forgive? The young mother felt hopeless that any of what the minister said was true. She turned to Charlotte, the only other person who really seemed to grasp the demon she had been fighting. She thought about her, wondered how she managed herself among church members, carried herself through the rings of suffering she encountered in those she felt called to serve.

She thought about Brittany's death and how she remembered only very little of the days following the tragedy, very little of who visited or what was done hour by hour. She had very little recollection of what else had occurred, where she had gone, what she had done. She had very few memories of the events. But she remembered Charlotte. She remembered how she stayed at the house for hours at a time, how she sat with her in silence, how she bowed without praying a word but somehow created a space to bring in some presence, some semblance of peace.

She thought about how it was the young and unconfident minister whom she called on that cold April night when she had run out of drugs and any excuse to keep living and how her pastor had calmly spoken of bringing over some coffee and pieces of cake and had promised her that she was not alone.

Nadine studied the woman. She tried to find signs of hope or faith, but all she could find was just another person struggling with what it means to lie down in the darkness and get up in the light. Another person who fought with demons and wrestled with grace. Another woman simply trying to find the balance in letting go and holding on. She saw somebody just like her.

"You believe any of that stuff you said?" she asked.

Charlotte pulled the blanket tightly around her shoulders. "I believe it now," she said. "Can't say I did yesterday or even if I will tomorrow."

Nadine nodded. She leaned her head against the wall behind her and appreciated once again her friend's willingness to speak honestly. As she closed her eyes she heard the last bell ring for the afternoon.

"That one yours?" the pastor asked.

"No, that's for the kids to come inside," she answered. "But I do have dinner in fifteen minutes." She said this as she lifted herself up and sat on the side of the bed.

Charlotte moved toward her and removed the blanket from around herself. She folded it and placed it near the patient. Nadine got up and stood at the door, opening it for her guest.

They walked out of the room and toward the entryway without further conversation. When they got to the end of the hall, they stood at the door of the dayroom.

The television was blaring some soap opera, and several patients were gathered on the sofa, watching intently.

The nurse at the desk glanced up and smiled at Charlotte. "You all have a nice visit?" she asked.

Charlotte waited for Nadine to answer, since she wasn't sure of a reply. "Very nice," the patient responded, then introduced her company. "This is my pastor, Charlotte Stewart."

Charlotte held out her hand to the nurse, who shook it.

"I'm Sheila," she said. "I've never met a woman preacher," she added.

She was young, looked athletic, and had perfect teeth.

"Yeah, well, they put their pants on just like the men," Nadine replied without emotion.

Charlotte laughed. "I'll be leaving you now."

The young nurse got the form for Charlotte to sign. The pastor took the pen and wrote her name and the time she was leaving. Then she handed the paper back to the nurse. A buzz went off and the first door opened.

"I don't know what I think about what you said," Nadine spoke to Charlotte as the pastor walked toward the door. "But"—she took a step and stopped, folding her arms across her chest— "today it helped."

Charlotte turned around to face her. "Well, today's all we got," she replied before heading to the exit. "So that'll just have to be enough."

Nadine followed her while Sheila came around the desk and stood behind her. Charlotte walked out into the second hallway and out the second door. She collected her purse and waved at the patient as she stepped through the final door and onto the elevator. Nadine watched the door open and close. There was a brief silence as the two women stood facing the entrance.

"You know you were moved to step 5 this afternoon," Sheila said to the back of Nadine.

Nadine turned around and stared at the nurse. Sheila knew that the suicidal patient hadn't cared about advancing, and she waited to hear the reply.

Nadine was slow but confident in her response. The air around them was brisk but still.

"Then I guess I will eat my dinner downstairs." She faced the front of the unit, closed her eyes, and took a deep breath as Sheila walked to the desk and opened the door in front of her.

"You need me to go with you?" the nurse asked.

Nadine felt in her pocket to see if she had any money. She had four dollar bills. She spun around to speak to the nurse and noticed Grandma sitting in a nearby corner, looking ready and eager for church. The young patient lifted her chin and faced ahead. "No, I think I'll be just fine." And she walked out of the unit, following her pastor, not at all sure of where she was headed.

Hope Springs Community Garden Club Newsletter

BEA'S BOTANICAL BITS

What to Do About the Weeds

Crabgrass, pigweed, clover, prickly vine—something is always growing in your garden that you didn't plant.

Mulching is the best preventive measure for weeds. But even layers of old leaves and grass clippings won't be enough to stop all of those ghastly intruders.

Hard work, ladies, nothing to do but hard work.

You can decide to let them grow alongside your lovely flowers or vegetables, taking up their precious air and space, or you can take action. Kill the mothers.

Be the happy hoer. Work out your frustrations on the roots and stems and brash leafy bodies of those unwanted garden guests, and discover a harmless way to deal with the troubles of your soul.

Ain't nothing like a pile of weeds yanked up from your flower bed to make you feel like a woman.

*J*essie poured herself a cup of coffee and sat down at the dining room table. Louise was going to drive them both over to Beatrice's, where they were having a sort of celebration of friendship before the event of Margaret's surgery. She was taking a minute to gather her thoughts before she got ready to go. She was ahead of schedule because she'd left the mill early. But she had discovered that in the last few days, since the news about Margaret, it took her a little extra time to prepare herself whenever she was going to see her friend.

At first she only thought she was anxious or sad about Margaret's news, that the shock of a cancer diagnosis in somebody her own age, one of her closest friends, had been the reason for her emotions. That what she was feeling was a natural and predictable response to hearing bad news about somebody you love. But then she realized that how she felt had more to do with what she knew about the disease and how it was that she found out.

Jessie had been the primary caregiver for her mother and an aunt on her father's side, both of whom had died from breast cancer. She understood how the tumor, once it has been discovered, could have been there for months or years, already splitting off from itself and aligning with other cells alongside it and even those in other places. She had seen how the tumor could duplicate and divide and move around into lymph nodes and fatty tissue and blood vessels and organs. She knew cancer was tricky and mean and could lull a person into thinking she was healthy and disease free, only to show up again in a new body part, with a new symptom, and a fresh approach to suffering.

Jessie ached with what she knew, the too-much information clawing at her, keeping her awake at nights and restless and distracted in the day. Her thoughts and dreams were fretted with the memories of her mother's last days and the way cancer inched into her body and into their lives and stole away everything they had of health and peace.

She struggled with telling her friend to start being in control now, to go ahead and have both breasts removed in the first surgery and to sign up for any experimental treatment, any aggressive chemotherapy or radiation that was available to her. To go ahead and have her family members checked for bone-marrow compatibility, since that process can often be arduous and painstakingly long. To start the fight now and to do anything and everything that was suggested by anybody in the medical community.

Jessie went through old files and folders and pulled out brochures and books and handouts and articles that had anything to do with the disease. She had, at least from during the time of her mother's illness, the latest statistics about survival rates and treatment options, names and phone numbers of experts in the field. And she gathered all these things to give to Margaret for her to examine. There were things Jessie knew she should share with her friend.

Then she moved from this kind of assertive thinking to the idea of just telling her not to do anything about the cancer. To sell her house, her car, her land, and do whatever she wanted—travel, spend money, visit family, just save what it would cost her for the medical and insurance company melee and not waste her time and energy, but rather simply live life any way she desired in the time she had left. That what Jessie really thought was that it didn't matter how aggressive a woman was, the disease was a death sentence and should just be accepted and lived with.

Jessie's mother had gone back and forth through five surgeries, drug therapy that left her insides ravaged and loose, radiation treatments that burned the back of her throat and the lining of her stomach, daily visits with a doctor who could never remember her name and who asked for payment up front, and excruciating pain from having lived too long. She died, of course, four years after the initial hopeful diagnosis.

"Her condition was farther advanced than we first thought," one of the doctors had said after she was shriveled and destroyed from the cancer and the cure.

The specialists acted as if the fight her mother had fought was honorable and to be commended.

"She was a courageous woman," a nurse had said.

"You should find comfort in knowing that everybody did everything that they could for her," another added.

But Jessie had not been comforted by this. It did not help her sleep at night, and it was not a reason to celebrate her mother's memory. Her mother had died sick and disappointed because all along she thought she was going to be healed.

Aunt Mary had fared no better, receiving only minimal care from the oncologist and the hospital since she was old and poor and black. In her situation, they would not even discuss possibilities for treatment. They had not even offered her chemotherapy or radiation. They just cut off her breasts and sent her home to die.

"Too far gone," a doctor said, like she was a drifting boat pushed away from the dock.

"Well, it's probably for the best," a nurse whispered, like death was her aunt's only possible blessing.

Jessie had never experienced such betrayal and disappointment, frustration and suffering as she did under the auspices of health care. She was still angry about things that were said, careless things that medical personnel passed out like their words might not be heard or counted. She was still mad about what they put her mother through, without learning what she wanted or how much pain it would cause. She tried to find ways to let her bitterness be taken from her; and she thought most of it was gone until she ran into it, harsh and unexpected, after she heard about Margaret. She remembered the things she had prayed to forget, and it tortured her to think that her friend could be facing the same fate.

She knew in the rational part of her mind that there were those who lived long, healthy lives after a diagnosis of breast cancer; her sister-in-law needed only surgery and had been discharged from her six-month examinations three years ago. She had co-workers who returned to their positions without any special needs, acquaintances who said cancer was the best thing that happened to them because it bolstered their hidden passion, forcing them to make changes in their lives that they had wanted for years but that, only after the diagnosis, had they taken the necessary action to see through.

All of these success stories she recalled and had set out for Margaret and herself to see, like cards on a table, these stories and the reminder that Margaret was white, which even if people didn't want to believe it, meant a higher survival rate than for black folks.

These were the things she had numbered off for her friend, counted them like they were evidences of the undisputed truth. These were the stories she told, not the others about her mother and Aunt Mary, not the other history.

But it was as if the mention of cancer cast her back to her mother's bedside, frenzied and threadbare. And she could not seem to pull herself away from the shadows of a time when nothing good had prospered. Hard but true, Jessie had no hope to offer her friend.

Even though she did not speak of them, would not tell of them, it was the surrender in her mother's hollow eyes, her frayed, ragged voice when she begged for the cool side of the pillow for her hot face, the way she breathed, frantic and flung, like a fish struggling to get back in the water, these were things that pressed against her mind when she thought about the cruel disease. And she did not know how to yank out or silence these thoughts, as they grew in secret places within her.

James Senior drove up and his wife didn't even hear him come in through the back door. He was whistling as he hung his jacket on the nail beside the washer and pulled off his boots, muddy from his walk through the fields with his son.

James Senior spent most of his days outside now; and the pace and the work pleased him. It was different from how he lived in Washington. There, even though he tried to garden or be out in his yard, the wind was always sharp, and the noise from the city drowned out his desire to dig or cut or grow.

He enjoyed his time with his oldest child, was proud of his love for the earth, a love that had passed from father to son for more generations than he could remember. He liked the long days and the restful nights. And he had almost forgotten how much he loved to watch the change of the seasons as they manifested themselves in the passing of time on the land.

He delighted in the seed of early spring, so tiny and fragile, as it lifted itself into the plush ripe height of golden summer, the spread of life so quick and full. The older man relished the season of the present moment when the soil was still warm and held promise of yield but the air was crisp and cool, the segment of time when the sun arched across the earth and sky, melting the green leaves into minature worlds of color. James Senior would close his eyes and smile when he remembered the way the leftover husks of corn fell into a silent earth, turning themselves into the food for next year's crop. He loved the frozen days and the silver glint of winter when everything stood still, barren and obedient, galvanized in an icy wait.

All of life was balanced in the nature of farming for the man come home; and James Senior and Junior walked or rode tractors across the rows of tobacco and soybeans, corn and strawberries, like the ground and the plants and the produce and the light and the rain and the green and the blue were theirs. Only and all theirs. And this life of seasons and cycles, death and resurrection, hope and promise, this was the only life of Hope Springs, North Carolina, that the two men, father and son, thought made it worthwhile to stay in the place they called home. It was so captivating, so possessive and possessing that James Junior never left it and James Senior, though he kept wanting to leave, could never seem to forget it.

He pulled off his socks and shook them. And when he leaned over, his hand balancing himself against the dryer, he cocked his head to the right and noticed something different about the small foyer. It seemed that the corner next to the shelves of old rags and detergents, the area just by the kitchen door, was empty. Clean and uncluttered, it appeared as if a new position had been made; and it struck him that it was as if something had been taken from its place. Something that once had filled it or lined it or swallowed it was missing.

Then, as he tried to remember what had been there before, what had rested there against the adjoining walls, he recalled the Saturday that he and Jessie had moved everything around. They left the wide open space as it was, deciding that this would be a convenient and easy place to stack the cardboard boxes that they began collecting and would use for packing their things for the move.

He considered at first that maybe she had taken them to the bedroom, that his wife, eager to get on with their lives in Oakland, had started packing without him. He thought that maybe she had left her job early and was planning to surprise him with how much she'd been able to accomplish in preparing for their departure. But when he turned to throw his socks on top of his boots, he noticed to his left that the boxes were broken down, the cardboard now lying flat in sheets, tied up with string and stacked on the bin that was used for recycling. He walked over and ran his finger down the sides of sixteen, maybe twenty, cartons. And as he walked out into the kitchen, he began to realize that what his wife had done was more than just make a decision about when or how to pack.

He stood next to the stove, saw the pot of hot coffee, got himself a cup from the dish rack, poured his drink, and went into the dining room and sat down next to Jessie.

She smiled at him as if to reassure him and patted him on the leg.

"You get the corn plowed up?" She took a sip of her coffee.

"Tractor broke and J. went to the store for a part."

Jessie nodded, but James could tell she wasn't really interested.

"You leave work early?" He wondered how she could have broken down and folded all that cardboard in only an hour.

"Yeah. I finished with the payroll about two and then the computer went down. Mr. Dixon told me to just go ahead and leave since there wasn't anything else I could do."

James brought the cup to his lips and blew across the coffee. He wasn't sure how he was going to ask her about the boxes. He knew they were honest with each other, always had been, even when the news was harmful. But for whatever reason, it troubled him to think she had made up her mind not to go with him, and he could not bring himself to ask the obvious.

As if she knew what he was thinking, Jessie answered. "We can't leave for California this fall." She sat up and waited for him to respond.

It relaxed him to hear her say we, and it was enough of an encouraging statement that he went ahead and asked her why.

"Margaret's got cancer." She had not told him before now. She hadn't known why. He had asked her what was wrong the night the women met at the house, but she had kept the information from him, thinking that maybe if she didn't tell anyone, she would wake up and it would have only been a dream. Since he had been busy with their son's farming and she had been working extra hours, it just hadn't come up when they had been together. She had not meant to keep silent about the news, it just hadn't seemed real enough to discuss.

"Is it bad?" he asked, remembering the stories he had heard about his mother-in-law and the conditions of others he knew.

Jessie shrugged. "Don't know," she answered. "Her surgery's tomorrow."

James nodded. He wanted to ask why a friend's medical situation would affect their plans to leave the state and didn't Margaret have sisters to take care of her; but he knew better. He was careful with sharing his thoughts about Jessie's friendships, delicate around any mention of the way she had managed her life all those years that he had been gone.

Truthful as they were with each other, he understood that his return to Hope Springs and into her house was unexpected and unnecessary. She had let him stay when he came back, without a hard eye or an undercoat of bitterness. But he saw how she was without him and recognized how she demonstrated a certain peace she had acquired regarding a choice not to depend upon what he brought to share. Since she had made herself into her own woman without him, without even the thought of him, the people in her life that she did care for and rely upon were not open for discussion or available for him to criticize. They both knew this, and he had commented on it only once.

He took her hand in his. "I'm sorry. Margaret's a good woman."

Jessie leaned into her husband, wondering how it might feel again one day to trust him fully, how it would be not to reach across the bed to see if he was still there. She wondered how it might be one day not to check the dresser drawers, the garage, the bathroom cabinet, just to make sure that he hadn't changed his mind, gathered up his things, and left again.

She had never stopped loving him or wishing that he might find his way home. For years, she wouldn't change anything in the house, in their room, in the closets, because she kept thinking that if he came back, it would need to be familiar, need to be the same as it had been when they were first together. She thought that if she kept space in the drawers and on the shelves, in her heart, that he would be drawn back to his life and the promises he had made and find the places once again where he fit.

Jessie believed he cared for her and would return. So when he did, there were still empty spots for him to fill. It had been a natural and easy homecoming. It had been a simple transition because they still loved each other.

But even love like that, clean and tidy love that survives wanderlust and middle age, love that doesn't play games or make believe it's something it isn't, even that love is tight around the edges and bears a protective coating, just making sure the heart won't swell to bursting.

When he asked her to go with him to Oakland, she knew that his first consideration had been to go by himself. She knew that maybe he hadn't stayed with the idea long, hadn't fought with it or agonized over it, had not really dealt with the consequences or possibilities; but that he had surely had it and that he had let it float about in his mind like a feather, softly tickling the thoughts and ideas she did not understand. She realized that he could have gone on his own, without her. And the fact that he didn't touched her, weakened her barrier of distrust. It was a gesture of companionship, and it pleased her that he had wanted to leave with her.

She was ready too. She loved this place that birthed her, reared her up, this farm that bore the prints and the bones of her great-grandparents. She loved the nearness of family and the casual unrestricted hours she got to watch her grandchildren grow. She was comfortable in her church and at her job, in her home, with her friends, and the way she had figured out a life for herself.

She had been happy before James came back, quiet, at peace, and happy. She had carved out a nice existence for herself that was full and satisfying. But Jessie was restless too. And even though he returned and moved right back into what he had left and she had closed herself around him, the restlessness was still there; and the thoughts of leaving town excited her in a way she hadn't been in a very long time.

There was a time when she wanted only to travel, to go to new places, different places. When she was young and rebelling, she considered leaving the country, changing her citizenship, living somewhere other than America. She liked the idea of speaking a different language, existing in a place where the rules were different from what they were in the southern United States. She relished the thought of living where she was not defined by her appearance, having her home in a location where skin color did not matter, where race was not the central issue. And in her considerations, she had even narrowed down her choices to France and Haiti and, of course, Africa.

The headstrong activist got married, however, and had children; and she stayed in Hope Springs, eventually even becoming comfortable in her home. She gave away her maps and travel guides and settled for what she had, where she was. But long before James's departure, long before they had grown old, Jessie and her husband had dreamed a dream together, agreeing with a plan to move, not out of the country, but out west.

They had spent countless late nights and early mornings, in the ease of a long hour, dreaming about the day they could leave

everybody and everything and pack up the car and drive across the
United States. They would stop, they had decided, town by town,
and meet the people, linger about to experience life in other places.
And they would go and go, up and down hidden highways, until
they ran into water, the paved road finished, the end of the path.
This would be far enough, they had thought. This would be the
new place to begin. And they would buy a small plot of land and
start over, discovering something new about California and the
west and the Pacific Ocean and themselves every day.

When James left her, she was devastated that he would run out
on her and the children. She questioned why hadn't he loved her
enough to stay. And she was angry, so very angry, that he would
give up on the marriage without even giving her a chance to
change his mind. For a very long time she was unable to think of
anything except how broken he had left her. And yet, the odd thing
was that, in spite of the anger and the disappointment, in spite of
the sorrow, Jessie managed to have a little peace. James left; but he
honored their dreams, their plans, and had not gone west without
her. He moved out of state and far away, but he had not gone in the
direction that had been created by the two of them together and
shared in the most sacred moments of marriage.

When he told her a few months ago of his sister's correspon-
dence and the idea he had for both Jessie and himself to leave the
south and go west, it pierced the older woman deep beneath desire,
way below regret, and stirred up thoughts and dreams she had long
understood to be smothered and dead. It pleased her to think about
their dream and how, even though the path they had taken had
become crooked and led them into places she never would have

expected, they were still heading in the same direction that they had imagined when they were young and spirited and in love.

"Are you very disappointed?" she asked, already reading and understanding the crease between his eyebrows, the way he was chewing on the inside of his lip as if he were making another plan.

James shook his head. "I'll just call Cleata and we'll figure out what to do about the property. I'm not sure we can afford to buy it without the money we'll make from the sale of this house." He sighed.

"But it's sure a good deal for California prices," he added under his breath.

Jessie could tell that he was thinking out loud, thinking and grieving.

He drew in his bottom lip and scraped it under his teeth. He peered out the window and watched the setting of the sun. He knew that his ideas about moving were impulsive and without real purpose. He knew that Jessie went along with him because she had always been the adventuresome type and had always wanted to leave home, but that they hadn't really thought it completely through. He knew that he and Cleata never had been that close anyway, and that he hadn't really considered what it would mean to move right beside her.

Wasn't one of her boys messed up with drugs? he wondered. And was his sister asking them to come because she was thinking that he and Jessie might become involved in some way, help her out, straighten him out, fix things? James hadn't thought about this before. Maybe they should wait a little and think this moving thing through before they just took up and left.

Maybe they should stay another year anyway and make sure Wallace and his young family were more settled before they sold the house out from under them and made them move into some tiny apartment in town. Maybe it was right, best, to reexamine this idea and decide if it really was the best thing for them. They had time, after all. Nothing was pushing them to leave now. Why not wait and think about it a little more?

But James knew himself well enough to know that it wasn't his style to think too much. He knew that stewing over some decision was like cooking meat too long. Hold something over a fire for more than a few minutes and it's going to burn away its taste. Plan on something too many nights and you're sure to strategize the life out of it. And he knew, sitting there at the table with the woman who had known him all his life, that scheming too much had been the reason he had left Hope Springs in the first place. The long, drawn-out plan to leave. The dream they squeezed to death.

In the beginning, it was delightful and sweet, easy on the tongue and smooth along the palate. They lingered in the bed every Saturday morning until well after the children had given up beating on the door and begging for breakfast. The young couple waited quietly, laughing to themselves, as the oldest child, in frustration, finally led the others away from their door and into the kitchen, where they figured out how to manage their own cereal and milk. And James and Jessie would lie in each other's arms, making love and making plans for what they were going to do when everybody got grown.

James would slide his fingers along the curve of his wife's back as he told her about how they would drive down the highway, windows down, Motown sounds loud and pulsing, and how they would stop at gas stations and truck stops and feed each other apple slices and lemon candy all the way across the country.

She would tease him like she wanted to sleep, pull the cover up to her chin and turn hard to the other side. And he knew that she was smiling because she was only waiting to see how long he could go before he slipped his hand under her arm and across her stomach and began to cup and caress her breasts. He would whisper from behind her as he slowly undressed her that the trip would be as good as the new life. He would talk of exploring and discovering new parts of the country as he stroked and gently kissed her all along and up and down her body.

James would talk about the rolling hills as he slid his fingers down across her hips and the heat of desert sands as he reached around and slowly felt inside her. It became such a pattern, such a lovely habit of their Saturday mornings, that Jessie began to equate lovemaking with a delicious journey and adventure that would end in a place different from the one in which they began.

He loved how they did that, week after week, a sort of ritual of desire and imagination. He enjoyed the dream and the layout of their departure from the life they knew as much as he enjoyed the sex; and Jessie grew to become as excited about his idea, their plans, as she did about his touch. And before too long, the intimacy and the play wound themselves together so tightly, became so entangled, that they couldn't do one without the other. Then the long, dull time of waiting began to fix them in the house and in the place where they were. And pretty soon they both became dissatisfied if he was unable to keep the plan new and stimulating.

The delight decayed and the sweetness thickened and hardened like syrup that's set out too long as life turned on itself and made them grow roots in Hope Springs. And they spent energy and money and time and too much thought trying to keep their children and their bosses and their parents and their longings pacified. Jessie grew uninterested and aloof when James was no longer able to add a new possibility or come up with something original about the trip or the move, and the dream finally began to wither and dry like flowers choked by weeds. It wasn't long before James lost the drive to think about life twenty years down the road, eventually dismissing the desire to touch and surprise his wife. And for reasons she couldn't explain, Jessie never tried to reignite the passion.

The dream grew stale and unfulfilling so that James felt as if there was nothing he could do except go away and maybe come back when the dream was dead.

The thought now of waiting a year or more, baiting the resurrected dream, trying to keep it alive with more ideas or more thorough planning, made James start to feel the same restlessness and discontent that had finally pushed him out the door and up north so many years ago.

Jessie looked at her husband. He was grayer, older; but she could see the beginnings of the faraway stare that had glazed his eyes twenty years earlier. She studied the lines that mapped his brow, the flap of skin at his neck, the stretched corners of his lips, and she tried to make herself think it wasn't the same gaze, the same resignation, the same disquiet that had ultimately pulled her husband away before.

She turned away and got up for more coffee. "Another cup?" she asked as she stood up from the table.

"Sure, if you got enough," he replied.

She nodded, took his cup, and went into the kitchen. She poured the coffee while she leaned against the counter. The thought of his leaving again crept up on her like poison in a garden. She steadied herself, her hands trembling, and tried to focus on the things she knew, the things that were rooted and certain, the things that could not be overtaken by storm winds or loose ground cover.

She had survived his coming and going before. She had a life in that town without him. She had family to care for and to care for her, and she had friends who would stand near her and guard the soft and seeping places inside her. She was not young and fragile anymore. She was not vulnerable to this kind of surprise. She was strong and mature and accustomed to disappointment. She was not going to go down again.

She put the coffeepot back in its place and reached in the refrigerator for the milk. She gave them both just a little, put the milk back, closed the door, and walked into the dining room as if nothing had changed, as if her mind had not just breathed in the breath of trouble.

"You all right?" he asked, noticing the flush high in her cheeks, the shaky way she handed him his cup.

"Fine," she answered, trying not to sound concerned.

"You all having something tonight?" He noticed that she had not changed out of her work clothes.

"A dinner," she replied, "for Margaret."

James nodded. The coffee had grown a bit cold. But he did not mention it or complain.

"There's leftovers on the bottom shelf in the fridge." Her voice was level, even.

"I think I'll go down to the cafeteria," he said, "think maybe I'd like a salmon patty." He turned to the clock and checked the time. "If I leave now, I'll get ahead of the old folks." Then he winked at his wife like everything was fine, like nothing was different, nothing had shifted. He drank down the last of his coffee and got up from the table.

"I'm going to jump in the shower." He headed behind Jessie and out of the room, calling to her from the hallway. "I'll see you later this evening, I guess." And he kept walking without waiting for her reply.

Jessie sat at the table and tried to fill her mind with hopeful things, solid things. She told herself that he was fine with waiting to move another time. She thought how he had come home, clear-eyed and at peace this time, how he had claimed that he missed her more than anything and that he was now better and happy to be with her after all those lonely years. She reminded herself that he was old now, had seen the world, and that they would live together for the rest of their lives, there in Hope Springs or out west in Oakland.

She thought of Margaret and remembered that the tumor had been discovered on a routine mammogram, an annual test that they had taken together, that she hadn't felt it first or been negligent with her examinations. Jessie knew that the statistics were in her favor and that her friend had all chances of a full recovery and a complete remission.

She thought that if he did leave, Lana and Wallace and little Hope filled up her life and would leave her no room for feeling sorry for herself or becoming lost to silence or pity. James Junior was nearby. Janice close. Robert just a phone call away. And she knew that Annie would be here if she asked.

"I will be fine," she thought to herself at first and then said it out loud, for confirmation and assurance. "I am stronger and better than I was before. I got history and I got support. I will be fine." She repeated this again as she heard the water turn on in the bathroom and knew that James was stepping into the shower.

She stood up from the table and saw Louise as she drove up the driveway. Jessie left her cup on the table and went over to the sofa to pick up her purse. She stopped at the mirror that was just by the door.

"You will not break my heart again, James Jenkins. You will not crowd my thoughts with bruised wishes and angry ideas that I should have done something different, could have done something different. This is my house, my mind, my heart. And you will not scatter your seeds of despair here. I will not let that happen. I cannot let that happen."

And Jessie left the mirror and the image of her strong self and walked out into the night even as the seedlings of disillusion were quietly growing in her heart.

Hope Springs Community Garden Club Newsletter

BEA'S BOTANICAL BITS

The Gardener and Her Tools

What kind of tools does a woman need?

I'm speaking, of course, about tools in the garden. You should have in your shed the following utensils:

For digging: a shovel and trowel.

For cutting: clippers, and perhaps a handsaw.

For cleaning: a leaf rake and a garden rake.

For irrigation: hoses and sprinklers, nozzles and such.

For hauling: a tarp and a wheelbarrow.

You will also want to invest in some good gardening gloves. Cotton ones for everyday use and a leather pair for the heavy work.

Don't be skinflinty about your tool purchases. It's better to spend a little extra money for a good rake than to buy a cheap one and ruin your back trying to hold it together.

And remember: A man may pretend he's the final word on garden tools, but it's the woman who knows the value of a sturdy hoe.

"*M*argaret, where would you rather lay down, on the sofa or in your bed?"

She wasn't sure who asked or even how she answered. She couldn't decide if she was at home or still in the hospital. And she didn't wake up and remember anything or feel clear and curious about herself until the light from the windows had disappeared and the brightness had faded.

Margaret saw streams of color when she first woke up at the hospital. Lines, wavy lines, of red and blue, yellow and green, that stretched down in narrow ribbons of velvet, dancing and twirling in the air above her head. She heard the sound of her doctor's voice, the nurses telling her to cough and sit up, the calls of Beatrice and Jessie, and the noises coming from herself as she apparently responded appropriately.

She floated in and out of rooms and the conversations in them, opened her eyes and smiled, took sips from the juice brought in after the initial postsurgery nausea, got in the car and out. But she always softened and fell back into the thin, cascading tendrils of color.

She started to turn on her side to get up and suddenly noticed a sharp pain that first pierced her chest and then rolled like electric currents out into her shoulder and down along her right arm. She lay back flat and waited.

There were women's voices coming from the other end of the house. Margaret tried to recall if it was the same night of the dinner they had shared, a night when all her friends had cooked for her and brought the meal to eat together, the night before the surgery, or if indeed the pain and the fog she felt were signs that she had already undergone the operation.

She tried to see where she was and began to claim for herself those things that were familiar. The worn quilt that rested on top of her, which was a present on her wedding day, porcelain figurines on her dresser that were gifts from her brother's wife for her birthday, pictures of faces she knew, Luther, her parents, a brown cedar jewelry box, handed down from her grandmother, and a tall china doll that she had bought at an antique sale.

She counted up the items, named them and where they came from, and convinced herself that she was finally and really in her bed, in her room, in her house. She was not at a hospital or drifting in some in-between world that was lit in colors; she was in the most peaceful place she knew. She was home.

"Hello," she called out, not sure how loudly she was speaking. "Hello," she said again, hoping she might be heard.

There was a rustle of bodies, a shuffle of feet and chairs, until finally four women were standing by her bed. They came to her like she had bid them to hear some all-important rendering of wisdom, some drawn-out last will and testament.

"Lord, you're finally awake." It was Louise. Margaret could tell by the gruff and attentive tone, the squareness of her body, the uneasy way she stood in a room.

"Thank you, dear Jesus." Jessie. That was Jessie.

"You want to get up?" Beatrice was already putting her hand behind Margaret's head to help slide her into a sitting position.

Margaret shook her head and just lay there a minute. Beatrice pulled away her hand and stood back with the others.

Only one of the women didn't speak, the youngest one. And without having to think any more about it, Margaret understood that the entire Cookbook Committee had gathered in her house, waiting for her to wake up, waiting to take care of her.

"What time is it?" she asked.

All the women checked their watches, the clock on the dresser, and like a choir answered, "Nine-thirty."

"P.M.," Charlotte added.

"What night?" Margaret asked, unsure of how many days had passed.

"Surgery night," Jessie responded. "Friday."

Margaret nodded, trying to retrieve the day that had passed. But it all felt like a blur, a series of snapshots of gloved hands, lists of rules about movements and exercise, medicine bottles, and cold, sterile walls. She was having trouble distinguishing dream from reality, memory from imagination; and she struggled with even finding a way to ask her friends what had happened.

As she was waking up, she reached over, her left hand feeling all the way across her chest. Her left breast felt normal and no different than before except that two or three pieces of surgical tape were stuck to it; and an ace bandage wrapped around her two, maybe three times. As she slid her hand across the right side, she noticed that there were several thick gauze strips, a long and spongy tube draining from under her arm, and the undeniable, flat, and revealing truth that her right breast was gone.

She took in a quick breath and the sudden wash of tears surprised everybody, mostly and especially herself.

Margaret wasn't sure why she was crying. She wasn't in pain. She didn't ache or feel grievous because she hadn't known what to expect. It was, she now recalled, exactly as the doctor had said it would be, all the way down to the number of pieces of tape and the size of the drainage catheter. It wasn't that she had been in denial or didn't understand what was going to happen. There was nothing out of place in the way the surgery had been explained and how it presently appeared to be.

But Margaret understood in that moment that everything was now out of place. She was unbalanced, abnormal, relieved of, dispossessed of, cut off from a part of herself that she had always had. Part of who she was and had always known herself to be was gone, missing, taken away. And the realization that her right breast had been forever removed from her and that she was not the same woman she had been less than twenty-four hours ago yanked her up from the ground of emotional stability that she had always operated from, leaving her rootless and defenseless while she was forced to fight with her sorrow.

"Oh, dear Margaret, sweet, sweet Margaret." Jessie dropped to her knees at the bedside and laid her head down at her friend's feet. She began to pray quietly.

Beatrice turned her face toward the door, unwilling to show her own sadness; but reaching out, she took Louise by the hand. And they stood there, side by side, tormented by what they thought they should or should not say.

Charlotte went around to the other side of the bed and lay down, easily, gently, next to Margaret. She did not pull the woman's left hand away from the incision and the missing breast. She did not say it would be all right or try to distract Margaret away from the things at hand. She just lay there, on her side facing her parishioner and friend, taking a tissue and wiping the tears as they spilled.

Margaret closed her eyes and in the postsurgical blur and in the sadness of her loss drifted back to the first time that she experienced physical intimacy. She was young, sixteen, eighteen at the most, and already had been thoroughly warned against the evils of flesh. Her grandmother, a devout and unswaying Baptist, had specifically told her what was and was not acceptable for a girl with pure and high morals.

Holding hands was reserved for couples who had been together for six months or more. A kiss was only after an engagement. A respectable young lady did not go out alone with a boy and would never sit too close to him or allow him to stand with her, languishing at the front door.

Telling jokes or crossing one's legs at the knees was unladylike behavior and was certain to attract trouble. No chewing gum or yelling was ever permitted, and ladies never spoke unless first spoken to. The virtuous young woman wore only dresses that began at the top of her neck, thick and heavy, covering her arms to the wrists, the hem falling at least to the ankles. There was to be no rouge or lace, no open-toed shoes or sheer stockings that allowed the delicacy of the foot to be imagined. There was an appropriate way to dress when courting, and it did not change regardless of season or age.

"A young woman," her grandmother had said, "has only two things to entice and eventually secure a husband. One is an unsoiled body and the other is knowing how to whisk a thick milk gravy."

Margaret, by the time she did marry, had achieved or retained only one of the two necessary virtues. She had perfected the gravy for sure, but a young soldier on his way to fight in Korea had been able to steal away her only other lure. Luther would be the one to enter her first, the one to introduce her to the complete sexual act of intercourse. But the soldier, the boy with eyes as solid and dark as wood, he had been the one to awaken the sleeping desires within her.

He was so confident of himself, so perfect in how he talked of his place in the world, how he eased himself next to her, his arm so deliberately and yet casually placed about her waist, that she had not even realized that what she had been guarding and protecting all of her adolescence could be so swiftly and easily taken from her.

He spoke of battles and combat, but his mouth was so soft, his eyes so tender, that without knowing it Margaret let the rules of her grandmother and the ideas of virtue slip through her mind and his fingers as she slowly lost herself in every word he spoke.

They met at a social, an event she had sneaked away to attend, but one that forever changed how she thought of herself and the way men and women discover each other in the curves and folds of bodies that are so unlike their own. They had only danced once, shared only one slow melding of lips and arms, one timeless moment of thigh brushing thigh, only one long rhythm that pulled them together and held them there, heart upon heart, breath against breath.

She had trouble even remembering his name now, his family or where he had gone to school. She could not recall how they met, who introduced them. She did not even know what friend had talked her into running out late at night and showing up at a party to which she had not been invited.

Lots of things she could not remember, dates, names, places. But some things could not be forgotten. Some things were not lost to time or squeezed out from her memories. Some things clung to the corners of Margaret's mind and would never be shaken from her. Things like the innocence in the way he held her, the soft way he slid his hand to the small of her back and steadied her there, her quickened pulse, and the manner by which he had lifted up her head carefully with the back of his hand and tenderly kissed beneath her chin, along the delicate bend of her neck, the ever so slight brush of his fingers across her tight and eager breasts. These were the things that neither time nor marriage could ever erase.

He had touched her first. He, in that one gentle, slow sweep across her heart, had let her know all the reasons her grandmother was so afraid, all the consequences of uncomplicated passion. In the time it took to dance to one easy song about love, he had moved the young woman in a way that demonstrated for her how it really feels to be a woman. He had made her come alive. And now, old and widowed, unheld and undesired, she raked her fingers across the barrenness, the flush and level place, and wept for what was lost forever.

"I'm sorry," she finally said when she was able to catch her breath enough to form words.

"Oh, honey, you don't need to be sorry." Jessie spoke for everyone there.

Charlotte, still in the bed next to her, began to straighten the covers around Margaret. Beatrice, her face pinched and red, turned around to face her friend and began to pat beneath her eyes and under her nose with a handkerchief she had in her hand. Louise dropped her head and stared at the floor.

"The surgery went really well." Jessie sat back and spoke clearly and with great care. She pulled her legs underneath her.

"Lou, go get some chairs for everybody." Suddenly, Margaret had gotten a hold on her emotions and was now concerned about everyone's comfort.

Louise pulled one chair away from the wall and set it beside the bed. Jessie got up and sat down in it, thanking her as she changed positions. Then Louise and Beatrice went into the kitchen and brought two more seats and sat down near the others.

Jessie was giving Margaret the details of the operation when they walked in.

"You'll need to leave that tube in for at least a week; but a nurse will come by tomorrow and show you how to measure the drainage." She reached out and took her hand and continued, "Are you hurting? Because they gave you some pain pills; and you can have another one if you want it."

Margaret shook her head. "Not right now. I'm okay." She took in a breath.

"How about something to drink?" Jessie asked.

Margaret nodded.

"I'll get it." And Charlotte rolled off the other side of the bed, tenderly, trying not to shake or move Margaret. She stood up and walked into the kitchen. "Anybody else want their drink?"

Beatrice replied. "You know, I'd like a little more of my tea, if you don't mind, and do you think you could put some more ice in it?"

Louise punched her friend in the side with her elbow. It startled Beatrice.

"What?" she shouted at Louise.

"Get up and get your own drink. This ain't the Golden Corral." Then she shook her head while she mocked Beatrice, *"A little more tea with some more ice.* Can you believe this woman?" She directed the question to Margaret.

Beatrice rolled her eyes and got up and followed Charlotte into the kitchen. "Well, she asked."

Louise relaxed in her chair and folded her arms across her chest. She seemed uncomfortable with the position, as if she had called attention somehow to her own two healthy breasts; so she dropped her arms awkwardly at her sides. No one seemed to notice.

"What did the doctor say about further treatments?" Margaret asked the other two women.

Jessie and Louise turned to each other and then back to their friend.

"What?" Margaret asked, not sure about what the glance had meant.

"You don't remember what your doctor said after the surgery?" Louise asked.

Margaret shook her head. She tried to think about the day, tried to recall what had happened, to whom she had talked, and the conversations she'd had.

"I do remember him coming in." She thought for a minute. "He sat down beside me, didn't he? Asked me if I wanted to stay overnight?"

Jessie nodded. "He seems like a really nice person."

Margaret tried to remember what he had said. But all she could think about were the rows of gleaming colors, the way they floated like tree branches all around her. She didn't remember what he had reported.

Jessie now realized that her friend had not been fully awake when the doctor had stopped by after the surgery. At the time she had appeared alert and coherent, had answered his questions about her level of pain and said she understood the postsurgical instructions and claimed she was ready to go home. Yet she apparently had been affected by the morphine or the anesthesia and had not comprehended anything.

Jessie was unsure of how to retell his observations and recommendations, was uncomfortable paraphrasing or repeating what he had already said so professionally. She knew that Margaret would be upset since they had all hoped the surgery would be sufficient, the only necessary method of intervention.

"They want you to do chemo." Louise blurted it out.

Jessie dropped her face away from Margaret's, but she did not let go of her hand.

"They're not sure about what the surgery found because the pathology report won't be in for a week or so," she added. "They took several of your lymph nodes to see if it shows up anywhere else. And he scheduled you for a bone scan in three weeks."

"It's not because they think something bad or anything." Louise sat closer to the bed. "It's just standard, to go ahead and do a few treatments"—she leaned her elbows on her knees—"just to make sure." She tried to sound reassuring.

Margaret nodded. She wanted to be optimistic.

Beatrice and Charlotte, finished in the kitchen, walked into the room.

"Here's you some juice." Charlotte moved between Louise and Jessie and knelt down next to Margaret. The older woman lifted her head, and Charlotte held the cup and straw in one hand and quickly slipped her arm behind Margaret's shoulders, holding her up while she drank.

She took several sips and then pulled away to let Charlotte know that she was finished; and she rested on the pillow. Charlotte helped her lie back and placed the cup on the nightstand next to her. Seeing no chair to sit on, she squatted down and sat on the floor next to Beatrice and Louise.

"Here, Charlotte, let me get you a chair." Jessie had stood up, but Charlotte waved her away.

"No, I'm fine here. Really. I'm young, remember?"

The older women agreed and let her stay as she was.

"So chemo, huh?" Margaret was trying to figure out what was ahead for her.

None of the women responded. Finally Jessie spoke up. "Oh, you'll be fine. It's so much better than it used to be."

Margaret turned to her friend, remembering the difficult time her mother had had, the many hospital stays and endless treatments.

"They have new nausea medication, a regimen of immune-strengthening vitamins. And the chemo itself really isn't as harsh as it once was." Jessie was confident.

"Mildred Lewis, from over at Liberty, she's been taking chemo for three or four months now, and she's doing real good." Beatrice drank some of her tea. "She didn't start losing her hair until eight or nine weeks into the treatments."

Louise and Jessie snapped their heads over to Beatrice, who suddenly realized what she had said. Charlotte stared at the wall and slowly let out a breath.

"Oh, right, my hair." Margaret then recalled the conversation she'd had with an oncology nurse who explained all the options a breast cancer patient would face. She recalled the discussion about chemotherapy. The possible side effects including infection, mouth sores, and ulcers. The usual side effects that were fatigue, lack of appetite, and the universally recognizable hair loss.

She knew then that her fight was only just beginning. And she turned away from her friends, wondering what resources she had to deal with the disease and all that went with it. She considered the equipment she would need, the amount of energy it would take, the close attention focused on herself and the changes she would undergo, the positive attitude she would have to have, encouragement, strength, faith. She closed her eyes, trying to decide if she was capable, ready.

The women were unsure of how to speak to Margaret, what to say or how to phrase their support. They inwardly wished for something to give her, some words of comforting wisdom, some meaningful talk. But they searched within their hearts and minds and found no such expression or advice. They had nothing to offer their friend but themselves; and sitting there in the room of sorrow and disappointment, it just simply was not enough.

Beatrice could no longer tolerate her uselessness. She sat forward in her seat acting as if she was preparing to deliver the most important proclamation of her life. She apparently had made up her mind about something. She rocked back and forth and then leaped to her feet, cleared her throat, and boldly announced to the women gathered around Margaret's bedroom, "Well, I for one am certainly not going to let you endure the chemo by yourself." It was a confident proclamation. She stood tall and straight, determined. Beatrice was resolved.

"Bea's right," Jessie responded, thinking she knew what her friend had meant. "We're going to go with you to your treatments, fix you healthy well-rounded meals, walk with you, pray for you, buy you those positive thinking tapes, whatever it takes."

"No, I'm not talking about all that." Beatrice was dauntless. She was clear and unwavering; and she moved across the room with a firm and steady gait.

"I mean we will not let Margaret go through this chemotherapy and the loss of hair by herself." Her words became muffled. The women could hear her fiddling around in the medicine cabinet, moving bottles and dropping things. Soon she opened and then slammed the bottom cabinet.

The other women glanced around at each other nervously, all too familiar with Beatrice's unorthodox ideas, her sudden leaps in decision making.

"Here's what I need." And Beatrice came in with a pair of scissors and a bag of plastic razors.

"Beatrice, what are you doing?" Louise asked.

"We're going to share in the chemo treatments before Margaret even has one." And she stood in front of the mirror on the dresser and began to open the new package. She pulled out several razors and laid them in a row. Then she folded up the package and set it aside. She picked up the scissors and, without saying anything else, began cutting her hair.

The women watched in horror.

"Oh my God!" the preacher called out.

"Have mercy," Louise said, like she really thought her friend was having a nervous breakdown and was needful of something divine.

"I think," Beatrice said as she continued to pull and cut, "it is our duty as her friends to share in this grief. I think we should let her know, let everybody know, that we are in this fight with her!" And the brown curls fell out and down.

"Beatrice." Margaret was speaking. She tried to sit up but was unsuccessful, and no one offered to help her since everybody was staring at Beatrice, completely in shock at what she was doing.

"Beatrice, stop. Really, this isn't necessary." And Margaret dropped against the pillow.

In a swift moment of clarity, Jessie swung around in her chair and peered at her friend in the bed. Then she pivoted her body to focus on the other two women in the room, Charlotte and Louise. She sat watching them for a minute, her gaze keen and searching. And then, as if she were lifted up and directed, Jessie got up from her chair and stood behind Beatrice. She took one of the razors, held it in her hands examining it, and then said as if she were under some spell, her voice gentle but firm, "We're going to have to have some soap and water, otherwise we'll get burns."

"You're exactly right. Why don't you go get a bowl from the kitchen, and I'll get the water warm and find some suds." Beatrice stopped clipping while Jessie went out of the room and into the kitchen. "Oh, and Louise, we're probably going to need some newspaper to put down on the floor." She noticed the floor around her feet. "I've already made a big mess."

Beatrice walked into the bathroom and turned the water on in the sink. Louise got up slowly like she was a child being ordered into the principal's office, obedient but afraid, and tried to find the newspaper they had brought in the room for Margaret when they came home from the hospital.

Charlotte stood up and began to pick up pieces of Beatrice's hair that had fallen onto the carpet. She brought around the wastebasket and gathered up the short, curly hair and threw the pieces in.

Beatrice came out of the bathroom, her hair butchered and chopped, smiling and satisfied. She went over and got a chair from the side of the bed and placed it directly in front of the mirror. She sat down and draped a towel around her neck and handed Charlotte the scissors.

The young preacher stood there for a minute, staring first at Louise and then at the image of Beatrice in the mirror. Then she shrugged her shoulders and began to crop more of the older woman's hair. She lifted and cut in concentration, feeling the soft strands as they collected and fell into her hands. And it surprised her how much she liked the way it felt to stand behind the older woman, engaged in such an intimate and ancient ritual as women cutting each other's hair. It began to draw her back to days long before, when she and Serena sat in their grandmother's kitchen, taking turns getting their monthly haircuts.

Charlotte was never actually allowed to cut her sister's hair, but it was her job to brush and comb it while they waited for their grandmother to get ready. They would arrange the kitchen, then she would take her place behind the stool where Serena sat, kneeling on a hardback chair. She gently removed barrettes and hair bows and began to pull her grandmother's soft-bristled brush through her sister's hair. They would play in the midst of this task

they shared, pretending that they were grown, sitting in a hair
salon like the places their mother went to get perms or waves and
color out the gray.

They would talk about movie stars and hemlines and hold
make-believe cigarettes in between their fingers and lips, acting
like the women they had seen, the conversations they imagined.
And it was a marking of the years for Charlotte as she could recall
hairdos and fashion and the way she moved from kitchen chair to
footstool to being able to stand directly behind her sister, able to
reach her in the same way she was now positioned behind Beatrice.

She loved her memories of those occasions with Serena; and
combing and cutting Beatrice's hair returned her to a time and a
place when she and her sister were safe and happy and delighted.

She cut as much as she could of the older woman's hair and
stopped. By the time Jessie had retrieved the bowl from the kitchen,
filled it with warm, soapy water in the bathroom, and walked into
the bedroom, Charlotte had done all the scissors could do. Louise
had placed the newspapers around the chair and was standing near,
watching. Charlotte moved away as Jessie placed the bowl on the
dresser in front of the women and took up a razor. She appeared
clear but somewhat unsteady in what she was about to do.

By this time Margaret had finally managed to pull herself up to
a sitting position in the bed. "Stop! Wait! Beatrice, don't do this.
It's all right. You don't have to do this. I know your support. I
don't feel by myself. Please, think about what you're about to do."

The two women faced each other in the mirror. The other
women pulled away. Beatrice was rooted, confident, and unafraid.
Her face was peaceful, her eyes shining. She spoke softly to
Margaret as her friend sat leaning in the bed.

"Margaret, please let me do the thing I most desire to do." And for a brief juncture she paused and then tipped her head at Jessie, who began to shave first the back, then the sides, and finally the front of Beatrice's head.

The landscape of the balding woman's face, the lines across her brow, the easy way she held her mouth, the calm in her eyes, none of these things ever changed. Nothing tightened or wrinkled, flushed or went pale. She did not bite her lips or even turn away. The quickening loss of hair did not diminish or disgust her. She never gasped or held out her hand to stop Jessie. She never closed her eyes. It did not shame or embarrass her or make her ugly. The cut and shave, in fact, seemed to do just the opposite.

The more hair that fell from her head, the more complete her baldness became, the more her scalp, white and unprotected, showed through, the more secure Beatrice appeared, the taller she grew in her seat, the higher she held herself. While everyone watched this vain and perfectly groomed woman lose her hair, sever this crown of designed and set curls, she was transformed before their eyes. Beatrice now understood the woman she really was. She had become exquisite.

One by one, Jessie, then Louise, and finally Charlotte, sat in the chair and gave up their hair and their thoughts about what marks a woman's strength. Individually and together they changed their minds and their hearts about the ideas they had always believed to be true.

They dismissed their long-held notions that it was breasts or hips or fair, slender necks. They knew it was something broader. They rejected their fears that they were not tall enough, not young enough, not slim enough, to qualify them as pretty. They understood it was something deeper. They refused their speculations that it was their husbands or their children or their jobs that defined who they were. Finally, they accepted that it was something more.

They denied what they had heard all their lives, that a woman is only a woman when she achieves the necessary sum of all her outward parts, that her worth is determined only by how she looks or by the appearance of her family. In this ritual of friendship and surrender they realized that they were so much more.

Margaret watched these brave and beautiful women from her bed. These friends that were to her like sisters gathered before her and offered up their sacrifice. She sat, fully awake, completely alert, and observed a ceremony of companionship and solidarity that touched her more deeply, held her more completely than had fears of dying or the pain of loss.

She rested there in her bed, her right side ravaged and amiss, while the women she called friends, women who had grown with her, aged with her, cried, argued, and laughed with her, women who were her courage and hope, her faith and strength, gave up their locks and curls, an offering to the cancer god, without protest or displeasure.

It was the loveliest thing she had ever seen or known; and later that evening, as the four friends took shifts sleeping in the chair next to her, their bald heads gleaming in the night, Margaret fell into the deepest and finest sleep she had had in weeks. She dreamed of colors, brown and black and silver ribbons, angel tresses, streaming from heaven, and pulling her up into the arms of God.

Margaret, unwhole and uneven, was at peace.

Hope Springs Community Garden Club Newsletter

BEA'S BOTANICAL BITS

Knowing What to Grow

What's a woman to put in her garden? Friends, this is your show-place, your stage, your land of self-expression. It is no time to be bashful or meek. The garden is no place for cowardice or timidity. Be brazen. Be haughty. Live on the edge.

You like flowers in early spring? Plant crocus and common snowdrop so that they sneak through the winter and give you a peek at warmer days. Want to show off to the neighbors? Plant shooting star and fleabane, lily of the Nile, and sweet pea. Let them grow unyielding and free, let them be your spirit.

Coneflowers and larkspur, pokeplant and marigold, let your hair down and go a little wild in your garden.

If it's vegetables you desire, fill the space with too many vines of cucumbers and squash, melons and eggplant. Don't be afraid to try something new. Peanuts and cow peas, Swiss chard and pumpkins. Get out there, ladies, go for it! It's time. Plant yourselves silly!

*N*adine came home to Hope Springs after a farewell lunch of spaghetti and hot dogs and a party with the other patients and staff. She was presented with brightly painted pictures of encouraging greetings and reminders to take care of herself and to be proud of how far she had come. Everyone gathered around to send her on her way with plenty of hugs and lots of excitement. There were chocolate cupcakes for all of them, baked by the nurses; and they each had a candle to blow out and make a wish for their friend.

There were general hopes for sobriety and good health. Two of the teenagers wished for her to have lots of money and great sex. The man who thought he was Jesus wished for her eternal peace; and Grandma, distracted by the basket of flowers Sheila brought for Nadine, wished for her color in her garden and that she, along with everyone at the table, would find salvation and quit smoking.

Several of them exchanged phone numbers and addresses, but Nadine was quite sure she would never contact any of them. It would seem too odd, she thought, being with these people out in a different setting. It would be strange seeing them again after all they had talked about and been through together. She felt like what they had shared needed to stay where they had shared it. To drag it into the outside world would somehow alter what had happened for her, what the experience meant. So she stuck the slips of paper in her pocket but knew they would never be used.

Nadine rode in the backseat as her mother drove. She did not want to sit up front, preferring instead to sit behind and be chauffeured.

"You hungry?" Her mother watched her in the rearview mirror.

Both of them worried that all that had happened, all the confrontation and therapy and tears and support, all of what she had given and received, was simply not enough.

Nadine blinked without a response.

"You want to stop and pick up some groceries or do a little shopping?"

She shook her head.

There was a pause as her mother drove, alternating between paying attention to the road and studying her daughter in the mirror.

"You know, you can stay at home tonight. You don't have to go back there right away." Her voice was stretched, thin.

Nadine stared out the window without answering, and her mother nervously cut her eyes away from her daughter and back to the road that lay ahead. The young woman rested her head on the seat and closed her eyes. She thought of walking again into the empty trailer where she lived, the silent walls, the vacant corners, the locked room where her daughter's things were still in place. She thought of how, in the past year, the space seemed to tighten around her when she was there alone, how the floor and the ceiling felt as if they were inching toward each other, flattening her between the grief of her own heart and the lonesomeness of space for a child.

She wondered if she would be able to stay there without running to her mother's, spending the night with friends, or checking into the motel where she sometimes worked as a cashier in the restaurant. She wondered if she should sell the trailer and move to another side of town, where Brittany was not so much a part of the landscape, where it didn't ache so much to breathe.

She wondered if what she had said she felt at her exit interview, strength and courage, could hold true when she was no longer in a place where she felt safe and protected, no longer in an unfamiliar place but returned to the environment that was wrapped up in her daughter's memories.

Nadine opened her eyes and watched as the cars raced past them. She saw the billboards and truck stops, the expressionless faces of drivers, the heads of children playing in their seats. She noticed guardrails separating east-bound from west-bound traffic, wildflowers growing on the banks of hills, trees, trimmed and tall, on the sides of the road. She caught glimpses of all sorts of life as they hurried past; and she did not know how to reply to the suggestion of her mother or to the unreliable possibility that staying away from what she had to face could help her or distract her in any way.

"I'd like to stop and see her." She spoke to the images flying by.

Her mother wanted to say that she did not think it was the best thing for the first day out of the hospital; but she did not know how to turn her daughter down. She only nodded.

The car slowed a bit. "You want to get some flowers?"

Her mother knew that she often stopped at a florist near the cemetery and picked up a few stems to put into the vase at the headstone. Black-eyed Susans, sunflowers, almost always daisies.

In the midst of her fresh and uncontrolled bereavement, this had been the one thing she had been able to manage, flowers at the grave and clear instructions to everyone else about what could and could not be placed there.

Nadine would not let anyone leave silk or plastic plants because she said it made the death and the pain and the memories artificial and that even if the flowers died before she could change them, that at least they spoke to the reality of what had happened.

Plastic flowers, she had said, created an image of stale beauty, an ideal of perfection frozen and bound; and Nadine understood there was nothing beautiful or perfect or frozen about her daughter's death. There was nothing beautiful or perfect or bound about her grief. It was what it was, ugly and completely imperfect, stagnant but alive; and she did not want to pretend it was anything else.

While she had been away, her aunts had kept the flowers fresh and changed; they had honored her wishes. But Nadine's mother suggested stopping at the florist because she thought her daughter might like to place her own flowers there, her own gift, regardless of what someone else had recently done.

Nadine nodded, thinking that she might get something different this time, something a little more permanent. And she began to wonder about what kinds of flowers grew late in autumn. She thought of the flowers she had seen lately, orchid-flowered dahlias and autumn crocus, and wondered if the florist had any of these or perhaps mums, as she might buy a plant instead of the usual cut flowers. She thought a bright yellow one would be nice since that was Brittany's favorite color and then wondered how a flowering plant would fare outside without constant attention.

Her mother drove the rest of the way in silence and then pulled off at the exit for the cemetery and parked right at the door of the florist. She turned off the engine and turned to face Nadine. "You want me to pick something out?"

Nadine unbuckled her seat belt and shook her head again at her mother. She got out of the car and went into the shop alone.

Nadine's mother sighed and rolled down the car windows. Nothing had changed between them. She wasn't sure what she had hoped for when she met Nadine at the front door of the hospital after she had been discharged. But she knew now, from the silence and the empty way she looked at her, that things for them had stayed exactly the same.

She had not known how to talk to her daughter since the accident happened, had not known how to convey her sadness or her concern, how to impress her love and support upon her. Even when the grief got out of hand and the drug use escalated and the despair widened, she had not known what to do or how to say it.

She had felt as powerless with her daughter as Nadine had felt when Brittany flew through the windshield and died in the preacher's arms. She was the mother's mother, the grandmother, the oldest in the line of tragedy. And she could not push away the sorrow. She could not lessen the doubts or put an end to the drifting away or relieve the slow dull ache of loss for her child.

All she had thought to manage was to take care of details, the bills, the cleaning, the filling out of forms, the driving to mortuaries and funeral homes, the phone calls to insurance companies and banks, those necessary tasks that had to be completed. These things and the wringing of her hands from the sidelines of Nadine's downward spiral were all she knew to do.

She tried to talk others into helping Nadine—Ray, the preacher, the family doctor—but no one seemed to know either what could keep her daughter from plunging farther and farther down and away. She grew desperate in her pleas, desperate in her search, but nothing she could think of or suggest was doing any good. She was afraid she had lost her oldest child for good.

She thought this hospital stay seemed different from the other times, that somehow what had happened behind those locked doors and stark walls may have been loud enough or strong enough or deep enough to keep her daughter away from the edges of death; but she was not sure. And she watched in a mother's uncertainty from the rearview mirror as Nadine slowly moved into the shop.

When she walked in, the bell on the door rang. The florist, the old man who had always been the one to wait on Nadine, yelled from the back that he would be right there.

Nadine did not respond to him but rather closed the door and went over toward the fresh plants that were situated in a corner near the window.

The man came into the room. He was wiping his hands across the front of his pants. He smiled at Nadine.

"Well, hello again," he said, recognizing her from past visits. "We've missed you around here. Where have you been?"

Nadine did not meet his eyes but did wonder who "we" was. She had remembered seeing just the one man by himself whenever she stopped to buy her flowers. She had always figured that he ran the shop alone.

She checked the price on one of the plants and did not give a lot of thought to her answer. "Just around," she said and then paused.

Then she decided to do something she hadn't done in a very

long time. She simply spoke the truth. "Actually, I've been in the psychiatric unit in Chapel Hill. I tried to kill myself."

She was surprised at how good it felt to be honest, how freeing it was to tell the truth; and she hoped that was a sign that she was doing better. Then she faced the old man, worried that she might have embarrassed him with her frankness.

The florist did not appear rattled at her response. He did not reply at first; he only dropped his head with a slow nod.

There was a long pause and Nadine thought maybe she should apologize. She waited as she stood just watching the old man, thinking he probably wished he hadn't questioned her; and then she changed her mind. He asked, she thought, and he got the truth. She turned and checked out an assortment of smaller green plants.

He spoke to her again. "What was it, a birthday? anniversary?"

He had come around the counter and was standing closer to her. He knew she always came in to buy flowers for her daughter's grave because he had asked her once before. They had not talked about the death; so he did not know how she died or how the young woman was doing with the loss. She always seemed clear and levelheaded when she bought the flowers. But he understood that what appeared on the outside was rarely a reliable indicator of what was going on inside.

The question surprised her. "Birthday," she responded quietly.

The florist was tall and thin, with a head full of white hair. The features on his face were soft but prominent, and his eyes were blue and clear. He stood there, in front of her, with his arms hanging loosely by his sides. He seemed sad but present; and he just held her there as he studied her, filling her with a strange sense of warmth and tenderness.

She became uncomfortable with the gaze and went back to examining the plants in the store.

"I've been there," he said in reply.

Nadine turned to him again. She seemed confused.

"Not in Chapel Hill, I mean. I was in the Veterans Hospital in Durham. I had a stint in the army." He did not take his eyes away from Nadine.

Nadine knew herself well enough to know that in past times she would have normally ended the conversation by telling him that she wasn't interested. She had heard enough sorry stories in her life and especially in the past few weeks, and even if his was more sorry than hers, more sorry than anybody else's in the psychiatric hospital where she had just been, it wouldn't, it couldn't, ease away her pain.

She started to tell him she only wanted to buy a flowering plant, a nice aster or cactus. But before she could say anything, he had started talking.

He rolled up his sleeve and showed a big scar on the inside of his left arm. "I was aiming for my heart, but I missed my chest and hit myself here." He pointed to the old wound just above his elbow. "Didn't do anything but scramble my muscle and get blood all over everything."

He rolled down his sleeve and buttoned the cuff. "Well, that and get myself locked up with a hospital full of crazy people."

"But I got some help," he said and walked behind the counter and started straightening up.

Nadine fingered the fern and the jade plant, thinking about what the old man had said. She was not put off by his scar or the easy way he had told his story. She appreciated his honesty, his willingness to share his own grief, and felt drawn to him in the way drunks are drawn to other drunks.

She walked closer to where he was standing. She reached up and touched him near the place he had shown her, high up on his arm, the healed wound of his attempt to die.

"You glad you missed?" she said after a bit. She watched him carefully, waiting for his reply.

"Some days."

She sighed, thinking that was not quite the answer she had wanted.

He pulled his arm away and gathered up a few pieces of green tissue paper that were left by the phone.

"And then some days I think it would have been best if I had succeeded." He folded the tissue and placed the paper in front of him.

Nadine stood near him and listened.

"My wife was everything to me." He said it like he had been asked.

"When she died I figured I'd never be able to be by myself, without her." He stacked a pile of forms together and put the phone book beneath the phone.

"And this place?" He glanced around the shop. "This is all her, everywhere my eyes land, it's Georgette." He ran his right hand up and down the scarred arm nervously, then stopped.

"Everybody thought I'd sell it after it happened." He shoved papers under the shelf and placed scattered pens and pencils in the plastic cup.

"I actually put the place on the market and almost sold it to her sister." He hesitated. "Then, I don't know. I kept wanting to be here and not be here. I'd run out of here after an hour, and then I'd get up in the middle of the night and drive out to this place just to sit in the dark. It was torture either way."

He shook his head and bent down to pick up some queen's lace that had fallen on the floor. He twirled it in his hands.

"I know some folks pack up everything and try to put the person out of their mind, try to get away from anything that reminds them of the dead. Makes the wound feel too fresh, I guess." The old man drew in a long breath.

"And I did try that. But I don't know." He focused on Nadine. "I reckon everybody does it different. There sure ain't no instruction manual on how to grieve."

Nadine smiled.

"So I kept this place. And somehow I like being near my wife, near the things that meant something to her. It's comforting in some strange sort of way, to carry on with the things she loved."

He laughed. "I suppose that ain't the way your doctors would suggest to you on how to get better." He winked at Nadine, remembering how the psychiatrists and nurses talked.

"But having this shop, remembering how she enjoyed arranging beauty, still doing her work, smelling her every time I handle a flower ..." He paused and then continued, "Somehow it keeps me getting up in the morning. Keeps me interested enough to stay living."

There was silence and Nadine didn't know what else to say.

"Some days are a hell of a lot better than others, though," he added.

A large transfer truck thundered by the shop and both of them turned toward the door.

"But today"—he faced Nadine and smiled—"today is a good day." He placed his hands on the counter and leaned on them.

"The sun is shining. I got fresh beautiful flowers. There's lots of orders to fill; and I got the grass mowed before the weekend."

Then he nodded at Nadine. "And I have a lovely lady come into my shop and want to buy some flowers." His smiled widened. "What more could I ask for today?"

Nadine blushed and lowered her eyes.

He waited a minute and then asked, "And what about you?"

She appeared confused, so he explained. "You glad you missed?"

Nadine didn't respond. She stared at the floor, her shoes, the pieces of tiny leaves strewn near the counter.

She thought about the moment when she stepped out in front of the car, the ease with which she did it. The resignation and desire to be finished. The hole in her heart, the one that opened when her daughter died, the one that was still there.

She shrugged her shoulders. "Can't say," she answered. "Too soon."

The old man nodded like he understood. "Yeah, it takes a while to decide," he said. "Give yourself some time."

Then he drew in a breath, tired from the depth of the talk they had shared.

He asked as cheerfully as he could, "Well, what kind of flowers are you thinking about today? You want daisies again?"

Nadine replied, "I think I want to buy a chrysanthemum, a yellow one, if you have it."

"That I do," he answered and walked to the room behind the counter. "I just got in some from the nursery last week. I've got yellow and this burgundy." He brought in two plants, both full of blooms and healthy.

Nadine moved closer to the old man and touched the flowers. "How do you take care of these?" she asked.

"Well, these are perennials," he answered, "which means, they should grow back next fall." Then he placed them on the counter. "Some plants are good just for a season; some last for years and years."

He realized he hadn't really answered her question about maintenance. "You just need to make sure they have good light and get plenty of water."

He spun them around and examined them. "They're pretty strong plants, so you shouldn't have any trouble." Then he laughed. "Kind of like me and you, can't kill them if you try."

Nadine smiled at him.

"Where you planning to put it?" he asked, trying to help her in her gardening decisions.

"One on the grave," she responded. "And I don't know. Maybe I'll take one home."

"Then plant the one at your house." He stuck his fingers in the pot. "You just dig a nice deep hole and place the entire base in the hole and cover it with dirt. Then water it good." He pulled out his fingers, which were wet and dirty.

"The one for the grave should just be left in the pot. I don't think they let you plant things out there." He folded the foil around the top of the pots.

"Which, now that I think about it, it seems kind of odd, don't you think?" He stopped. "I mean, you have to plant your loved ones there, right? Why not have some flowers to grow on top of them."

Nadine agreed. She too had thought that such a policy was

ironic and remembered saying so when she was told about it at the time she bought Brittany's plot.

"So what color will you have?" He shook the dirt from his hands.

"Yellow," she replied. "And I think I will take two." She stood back. "Maybe I'll plant one by my front porch."

The old man nodded and returned the burgundy plant and brought out another yellow one. Then he held out his hand. "By the way, Walter's my name," he said.

"Nadine," she answered. "Nadine Klenner." She shook his hand.

"Well, Nadine Klenner, in honor of your release from the hospital and your failure at suicide, consider this a two-for-one special. And I'll even throw in a few stems of your daughter's favorite flower."

He walked toward the large cooler around the corner and brought out five stems of daisies. Then he wrapped them in the green tissue paper. He rang up the charges and took Nadine's money.

"Will you need some help carrying these to the car?"

Nadine shook her head as she stuck the cut flowers under her arm and picked up the two plants.

"It was very nice to meet you, Ms. Klenner," he said as she walked to the door.

"You too, Walter," she replied. Then she turned to him and asked, "Oh, by the way, how do I know if I'm doing the right thing for these flowers?"

He smiled. "You're taking them with you, aren't you? Giving them a space to grow?"

Then he added, "Though I certainly can't say for sure, I expect that a choice of life, even if it seems like a small one, is always the right thing."

Nadine said good-bye and then walked out of the little store and headed for the car.

When she got outside her mother met her and took one of the plants from her hands.

"I was getting worried about you." She opened the front door on the passenger side.

Nadine placed the plant on the floor and the daisies on the seat. Then she opened the back door and got in. Her mother set the other mum down, closed both doors, and walked around to get in on the driver's side.

"I was talking to Walter." She reached her seat belt around herself. "He wants to die, too."

Nadine's mother gazed at her daughter in the rearview mirror, unsure of what she meant.

Nadine faced the road ahead even though she knew she wasn't driving and didn't need to watch. She thought about the man and all he had said. She thought about his wife and how it must have been for him when she died. She thought about keeping things like they were, leaving things as they were before somebody died, and wondered if that was the right way to live, the best way to go on with life.

She wasn't sure if she should keep Brittany's room like it was, locked up and untouched, or if she should pack up everything and move out. But then she thought again about Walter and the shop, and she realized that he hadn't really done either of those things.

He had kept the store, but not kept it like it was. Nadine had noticed that there were new things in the shop, seasonal items for holidays, different kinds of plants, and fresh paint. He had not left everything as it was before she died. He had been willing to keep her place contemporary and up-to-date.

And yet, he had also not changed everything either: the coolers and the shelves appeared to be old, part of the original store. He had kept a lot of what had been there that his wife had designed and organized, but he had not left it only and exactly as it was.

Nadine thought about it and understood that Walter had managed a sort of middle-of-the-road grief. He had not decided on one extreme of enshrining his wife's memory nor had he chosen the other extreme of wiping away everything she was. He had pulled them both together, somehow finding a way to honor the things she enjoyed and incorporating those things into his decision to survive. He had figured out that blending her life and loves into his life had helped him go on; that by continuing to love her, deepening, even, his love for her, he had discovered the answer he needed in knowing how to stay alive.

When they got to the cemetery, Nadine got out, taking one of the plants and the daisies, and walked to Brittany's grave. Her mother stayed in her seat and did not even ask if she should go along. She decided that Nadine had planned to do this and needed to make this visit alone.

There were fresh flowers in the vase, and Nadine stuck the daisies in with the cornflowers and lattice her family had brought and then arranged them. She put the potted mum next to the vase and checked the soil to see if she needed to get it water. Since it was wet, she pushed it back against the headstone; and then she sat down on the grave.

"Hello, Button." She smiled, remembering how Brittany liked that pet name.

"I'm sorry I've been away." She thought about how many weeks she had not visited. She pulled at the grass around the grave.

"I guess if you've been allowed to watch, you've seen how crazy I've been."

A flock of geese flew over her head on their way to the lake behind her, in the other section of the cemetery. They were loud in their flight, and she stopped to listen to them.

"I'm sorry, you know." Nadine talked to the stone, the letters of her daughter's name chiseled into granite. She reached up and traced the words.

"I was wrong not to buckle you in a car seat. I was wrong to leave you so much. I was wrong not to know how to save you. And I was wrong to pull you away from your daddy." She stopped and took a breath. The clouds moved effortlessly across the sky, and she noticed a narrow line of color down at the fence on the edge of the property, a stream of pansies, planted and growing.

"And I've been wrong ever since. My feeble attempts to die have done nothing but brought shame to you and your memory." She hesitated. "And if Charlotte is right, and you knew about this, then I've brought sadness into your new life. And I'm sorry for that too."

Nadine turned around and leaned against the headstone. She lay on the grave of her daughter and peered out over the cemetery. She watched the birds settle on the lake, the leaves twirling off the branches and floating on the autumn breeze. She saw the countless other markers, each with its own flowers or balloons or flags, the even grass, and the smooth slope of earth. She thought about Walter and the things he had said, the way he had figured out for himself how to survive.

She thought about Brittany and the things she had loved, the things all little girls love, picnics and stuffed animals, wide open spaces and bright, sunlit days. She thought about her daughter's heart and how she had always cared for other children who didn't have as much as she had, how she would sneak into her room at Christmas and bag up a few of her new toys to give away when she heard about a fire or tragedy that meant someone wouldn't have gifts.

Nadine realized that if she wanted to do as Walter had done with Georgette, keep Brittany alive by continuing to be involved in the things she enjoyed, then she would have to figure out how to open her own heart, learn how to love, purely and without complications.

"It would be easier to run a flower shop," she said to the cool stone behind her. "Doling out roses is a whole lot less trouble than trying to grow the heart of a child.

"But," she said to the blue sky and the silent ground beneath her, the birds and the dancing gold and red leaves, "if I'm trying to stay alive, trying to keep my soul from dying, I guess there's nothing better than learning how to grow some kind of love."

She turned and looked down at her daughter's name, the angel that was engraved at the top, the dates of birth and death, the final declaration of a person's life.

Then she whispered, "I wonder if it only lasts a season or if it'll come back next year."

Then she remembered what the old woman on the psychiatric floor, Grandma, had said once when the nurse asked her why she was always going to church.

"I'm expecting to be with the redeemed when the seed of God's love bursts open," she had said. "But even if I'm walking through the fiery halls of hell, if I'm spreading the news of Jesus, I will not be overlooked."

At the time Grandma had said it, Nadine had thought the old woman was speaking nonsense. But now in the fullness of the sun as she sat near the remains of her only child, it actually seemed to make sense. She thought she understood what the old woman had meant.

You keep looking for what you need to find. You can't ever really be sure it's going to be like you think it will be or even if you'll recognize it when you see it. You can't be sure what you plant today will grow next harvest. But that doesn't matter, you just keep planting in hopes that something will one day show up.

Nadine pulled herself up from the ground, touched the flowers, the stone, and the earth that covered her daughter. The childless mother emerged from the grave, stronger and less afraid. And though she still stumbled, she knew one day she was bound to find her way.

Hope Springs Community Garden Club Newsletter

BEA'S BOTANICAL BITS

A Changing Garden

Sometimes our gardens can mirror our lives. We've grown old and boring, always planting the same things in the same places, expectant of the same blooms every year. Maybe it's time to change things. Maybe this season is the time not just to divide the bulbs but to remove them completely and put them somewhere else.

Maybe you need a soil overhaul. Till in a new compost pile or bags of manure.

Maybe you need some fertilizer. After all, that always delivers a little spice to your beds. Adding a bit is like putting Viagra in your husband's medicine cabinet. Firm and plump vegetables always make for a livelier dinner.

Try new planting ideas. Rework your borders with stones or straw. Plant something new in an old garden. Switch things around. It might be just the time to surprise yourself with a new spark of life.

When Jessie came home bald and without an explanation, James looked up and thought it was Ervin, her older brother, coming through the front door. It took him a minute to try to understand what Ervin was doing in Hope Springs since he had been living in Alabama for more than thirty years. He couldn't figure out why he was in Jessie's house, having come in unannounced and without knocking. And then he noticed the dress and the gliding of her hips from side to side and he knew it was his wife.

He jumped up wild-eyed and alarmed and shouted out "Holy!" without finishing the expletive, and then, "Dang, woman!"

The newspaper was thrown in the air, the recliner swung back and forth as if he were still in it.

Then, after a brief pause, he left his stance of surprise and walked closer to her, taking in her round and perfect head.

Finally he asked, "What kind of group are you women?" And he reached up and slid his fingers down along the slope of her scalp.

That was all he could think of to say, that and a sort of sucking noise he made as he drew air in through his teeth.

Jessie closed the front door and locked it, set her purse on the narrow table at her left, and hung her keys on the hook by the framed mirror.

"We did it for Margaret," she said briskly and without further rationalization.

She walked by him nonchalantly and proceeded to the bedroom where she began taking off her clothes.

James followed close behind her, then stood at the door.

"She asked you to do that?" He still seemed to be in a state of shock.

"No. We just decided to do it." She yanked off one shoe. "So she won't go through the chemo by herself." And she threw off the other one.

James walked into the room and stood in front of her at the dresser, shaking his head as he peered at her bald head.

There was a minute of silence.

"Well, quit staring at me," she said. "It's like you haven't ever seen the top of my head."

"I ain't ever seen the top of it looking like that."

He grinned and folded his arms across his chest. "This is something." And he made a humming noise that reminded Jessie of old men chewing on fresh news.

He cupped his chin in his hand and just watched.

"You better be glad your mama ain't here to see you. It wouldn't have mattered how old you are, she'd have whipped you for that."

Jessie pulled off her panty hose, shaking her head even though she knew her husband was right. Her mother wouldn't have seen anything loyal or heroic about this act. She would have been appalled. Hair and its style were of utmost importance to her.

Jessie remembered that as a younger woman, her mother spent a lot of thought and energy on the appearances of herself and of her children. As an older woman, she would not allow anyone in her room without first having the opportunity to comb and fix her hair. When she lost her hair to chemo, she would never go anywhere, not even to the bathroom in her house, without first having one of her many wigs perfectly placed on her head.

And even when her children were old and grown, she would not hesitate to remind them of the latest hair products or what they could do to appear more refined. "I hear Afro Sheen has a new gel that smells like perfume, no more lye," she'd say while she fingered her son's curls. Or, "You know, you can soften that with a little baby oil."

If she were alive and had seen Jessie's head completely shaven, shiny and picked clean, her daughter out in a public place, uncovered and unashamed, it would have disappointed her beyond words.

"A woman's hair is her crown" Jessie remembered her saying. And then she would call her daughters in the room one at a time and straighten their hair with grease and a hot iron. It was an exhausting and elaborate affair for the girl children in her mother's house. And they fought it and rebelled against it, but their mother always won. She was going to tame their unruly hair.

She wanted them to have perfect tresses, unmatted and soft, she would say. "Like white girls," Jessie and her sisters would complain. But it would not matter. The mother always got what she demanded, and Jessie recalled the long hours of hard and painful work it took to bring her mother's idea of perfection to the tops of their wild heads.

She'd pull and comb and pull and comb; and then when she wasn't washing or straightening, burning their scalps with homemade soaps and foul-smelling lotions, she'd wrap their hair up in old panties and pieces of torn pillowcases or cleaning rags. They hid in their rooms most of their childhood, fearful that someone would stop by to visit and see them. And they whined to her every chance they got that none of their friends had to go through such an ordeal. But it didn't matter; Jessie's mother never allowed her children to have knotty or natural hair.

When her youngest daughter had come home from college with an Afro standing five inches from her scalp stretched and full, her mother had been more upset about her hair than she was about the arrest record from her activities in civil disobedience or the smell of tobacco on her breath.

Jessie could still remember the disgust on her mother's face when she walked in the house after being gone for almost a year. She did not hug her or welcome her home. She did not clap her hands or offer up a testimony of praise. She simply stood back from the door, turned her face away, and spoke to her husband like Jessie wasn't even there.

"The child's been dancing with the devil," she had said, as if the length of Jessie's hair, the style or lack thereof, had given full evidence that she had fallen headlong and unprotected into the arms of evil.

Jessie smiled, remembering her mother's discontent. "Oh, she'd understand." And she lay back on the bed, spreading out her arms, knowing it was a lie.

"She wouldn't understand that," James replied.

And Jessie knew the truth had been spoken.

He sat down beside his wife and she leaned against him. He laughed at what she had done and then began scratching her scalp. It felt good to Jessie because her head was dry and already itching. She lifted and turned, resting her neck across his lap, so that he could massage every spot on top and all along the sides. She closed her eyes, loving how his hands felt upon her.

It reminded her of years long past when they would lie together, the whole family, a bed of children, taking turns rubbing and scratching each other's heads. It had been the Jenkinses' familial means of affection that they had shared with each other. The late-night ritual that unburdened them from the day of trouble, unleashed them from the tight restraints of the unfair world, eased them into the night of safe rest and perfect dreams.

It was the faultless combination of finding love and sharing love. And the only way any one of them could receive a massage was to give one. You scratched and you got scratched. And it was generally accepted that you got only as much as you gave.

"Baby, you're making this too good." She turned to the other side. "I'll be too sleepy to pay you back."

"Well, we can put it in a rain check," James said as he sat against the pillows. It pleased him to see that his wife was relaxing.

"Where are Wallace and Lana?" she asked, suddenly noticing that the house was unusually quiet.

"They took the baby and they all went to stay with Janice tonight. Something Wallace has to do early in the morning about school, I think." James couldn't remember exactly what his grandson had said.

"So, it's just us here by ourselves?" Jessie opened one eye when she asked.

"I think that's about right," James replied as he began to move his hands down along Jessie's neck.

"Been a long time for that."

He tickled her under her chin and agreed.

"You know, you're kind of sexy bald," he said as he studied the honey-colored flesh, the smooth curve of her skull dipping into her neck.

And Jessie laughed, enjoying her husband's interest. "Yeah, well, you're kind of sexy bald too."

James glanced up in the mirror realizing that it was true, he had lost most of his hair. He turned and examined his own appearance, thinking he didn't look quite so bad himself, even though he was old and thin-headed.

Jessie sat up and situated the pillows behind them both, then lay beside James. She knew they needed to talk some more about what they had started the night when she had left to go to Margaret's. But she was hesitant, anxious that what she feared might come to pass.

She worried that he was already packing his things, already filling the car with gas; and the thought of his leaving hemmed in her desire to know for sure. She almost preferred not talking about it, not discussing it, just coming home one day, unknowing and unknown, to discover his departure, having things happen as they did the last time. No conversation or wishes conveyed. Just a note on the table and the house suddenly still.

She took in a deep breath against her better wishes and asked, "What did you decide about the move?"

She was straightforward but nervous. And she sat up completely.

James noticed the shift in her body, the tightening of her brow and spine. And he paused and took his wife's hand into his, their fingers folding over one another and interlacing.

"I didn't decide anything," he said reassuringly, pulling both of their hands up to his mouth, softly kissing hers.

"I thought I'd call Cleata later this week and check on the house. See if anybody else has made an offer. See what she thinks about us waiting."

Jessie inched closer to him, loosening up a bit.

"But then, I don't know, I thought about it and maybe we shouldn't live that close to family. Maybe we should search around other places some."

He kissed her wrist and moved his lips up her arm.

Jessie appreciated the attention she was receiving and liked the thought that for the first time since James's homecoming they were staying in the house by themselves. For the first time in many years her house was quiet, but not lonely; the door to the bedroom, open and welcoming, with someone already in.

And now for the two of them, together after such a long time apart, there was no fear of being discovered or interrupted or silenced. It was just them.

"Maybe we should just stay here and spend all our money on a very long and expensive trip," he whispered to her.

She was drawn to his suggestion.

"We haven't got to abide by the old dream," he said as he began pressing his lips along the outside of her arm and up across her shoulder.

"We can make a new one." And he reached up and unzipped Jessie's dress.

She felt his hand slide inside her dress, and she positioned herself so that she could come out of her clothes more easily. And then something odd began to happen.

The night began to feel like past nights, like sweet nights when they were young and passionate and in love with the world and each other. The moment, as he began to unsnap and unbutton, began to pull her back into a time long gone when she and the man she married were the only two people in the world, when how they touched and kissed and moved together, this dance of love, had been all that mattered.

She lay down beside him, gently.

And he began to dream.

He whispered into her ear about the breeze blowing near them, calling them, leading them into a faraway place, a long and foreign adventure. He said that the old way had passed but that a new one lay ahead of them.

She closed her eyes and listened.

He stroked his fingers across her while he talked about flying to find it and sailing to feel it and driving down highways and country roads and city streets to reach it.

"Out past state and border," he said as he stretched her arms above her head.

"Beyond usual talk and common schedules." And he pulled off his own clothes, lying beside her, body touching body.

"Far from ordinary." He felt her lifting herself for him.

"It's a new way."

And slowly, easily, knowingly, he talked of a land of long, narrow grasses and white burning sands. He spoke of low streams and wide, deep rivers that they would rest themselves near, cool themselves in, and listen to as they followed where they flowed, gliding toward the dream that rested at the lip of an ocean, a faraway ocean that had bathed the visions of lovers from long ago.

He whispered to her of women who walked with broad golden baskets on their heads, sisters tall in grace, men with long, taut legs and voices deep as thunder. He talked of lions and elephants and slender yellow giraffes.

He spoke of wild painted horses that ran freely on open plains and water animals, slippery and gray, that grew as big as the lakes. He talked of lush green jungles and miles and miles of nothing but pulsing, living, sacred space.

He talked about places she had never heard him say, names on maps she had thought only she had touched with a fingertip, places she had envisioned but that they had never discussed, new places, different places.

Places in the motherland, her motherland, places from long ago in her hidden memories, places she had dreamed of herself so many years ago that she had only thought of them as pretend, imaginary. Places she held on the tip of her tongue but never claimed, never spoke, never declared.

But when he called their names, like old, forgotten friends, Kenya, Nairobi, Zambia, and Lusaka, she rose up to hear them, rose up to meet them, rose up to speak them, as if she had landed in a place of home.

A place that spoke to her so deeply, reached within her at such a depth, she drew him closer to her, pulled him on top of her, opened herself to receive him just so she would hear him say the names of towns and villages she knew but had not remembered. Family she had heard of but never met.

He lay upon her and filled her with a different dream, an ancient longing, a forgotten imagination. And she took it all inside her, all of him inside her. And for the first time in a very long time, that which was old became new and the thing that was new had suddenly become as old as life itself.

They were going to Africa.

The lovely dream, the new dream, was now no longer a means to escape the world they lived in. It was no longer a way only to silence the cries of hungry children or soothe the lawless longings that haunted fading youth.

This dream was the merging of many dreams, the blending of going away and coming home, the mingling together of hope and promise, of steadfast assurance.

And Jessie's heart was bathed in the warmth of confidence, a quiet rhythm of expectant gratitude.

James was home to stay.

Hope Springs Community Garden Club Newsletter

BEA'S BOTANICAL BITS

Keeping Your Garden Growing

Ladies, gardening friends, no matter what kind of garden you grow, you need to provide continuous and proper care. Gardens are like relationships: to keep them healthy, you have to stay involved. You have to show a little interest.

Bulbs should be separated. Trees must be pruned. Weeds have to be pulled. Mulch has to be added every year, and crops need to be rotated.

Suitable irrigation, ample light, protection from the extreme heat or cold, these are all imperative.

You want to keep growing beautiful plants, don't you? You want to be the envy of all your gardening neighbors, right? Then, sisters, get out there and get to work. The garden is always waiting.

*C*harlotte had an appointment with Marion the day they were all going with Margaret to the doctor to hear the surgery findings and get the schedule for her cancer treatments. She had managed to work it out so that she could leave the therapist's office and meet them at the doctor's.

After several sessions, she was feeling better about her decision to talk with someone. Over that brief period she had begun to develop a deep respect and appreciation for the woman who listened to her. And that was mostly what Marion did, just listen. She offered only an occasional bit of counsel or helped Charlotte form a framework to understand her feelings and her longings.

The young woman had spoken about her parents, her disappointing childhood, the responsibility of taking care of her younger sibling, her grief over her death, and the lack of real opportunities or permission to play.

"Too serious," Marion had said and questioned if Charlotte had ever taken a class or gone on a trip that was meant only to be fun. Her assignment for this session was to think of something she wanted to do, a fun thing, a playful thing, and they were to discuss it as a viable option for the near future.

Charlotte had thought quite a bit about the idea and was actually considering adding something different in her life. A vacation or going back to school, something or someplace that would bring a spark into her life.

When Charlotte got to the office door, Marion waved her in without noticing her. The pastor walked beside her and sat down on the sofa.

"Just finishing up a note to myself," she said, still focused on the pad of paper in her hand.

Charlotte didn't speak.

Marion got up and moved around the desk. She did not look at Charlotte. Then she walked to where she normally sat. When she did finally see her client, now completely bald, Marion fell into her chair.

"Oh my God, you joined a cult!"

Charlotte laughed. She was starting to get used to the stares and odd comments because it had been a week since the women had shaved their heads.

"No, just the church."

Marion knitted her eyebrows and waited for more.

"For Margaret." She hesitated to see if Marion would remember her conversation about her parishioner. "The one with cancer."

"You did this by yourself?" She got up from her seat and sat down next to Charlotte and rubbed her on the top of her head, something everybody seemed to want to do.

Charlotte shook her head. "No, it was sort of a group decision." She sat back on the sofa. "Seemed like the right thing to do at the moment."

Marion returned to her seat slowly and sat down. "Does it still seem like the right thing now?"

Charlotte thought for a minute. She wondered if there had been a hint of disapproval in Marion's voice. But then she realized that was not her therapist's style, so she simply thought about the question.

When it had happened, when Beatrice had started cutting her own hair, Charlotte had felt embarrassed for her and thought she would cut hers as well, just so the older woman wouldn't have done something so drastic by herself. It would be an act of sympathy for Beatrice more than for Margaret, because Charlotte wouldn't be able to watch her parishioner stand boldly alone. That was simply how she was and she knew that about herself. Even though she had thought it was a lovely act of solidarity to stand with Margaret in her sickness, she was mainly going to do it for Beatrice.

Then, when Beatrice had handed the preacher the scissors and she had started cutting, cutting and remembering, she realized that she was engaging in this act for herself. She really wanted to shave her head. She had not known how to explain it except to say that she wanted to share in a friendship with Margaret and with Beatrice; and she wanted to mark a date for herself, ritualize a beginning when she would demonstrate a letting go of some things in her life, a moment, a day, when she would try to start again. A life, a new life of something more than just survival, a life of health and courage and freedom. That just as Margaret was making decisions to take care of herself, to fight disease and overcome cancer, Charlotte was making a decision to take care of herself, to be more patient with herself, to ease up a bit.

She turned to Marion to answer her question about whether or not she still thought the shave was the right thing. "Absolutely," she said with great resolution. "I like the cleanliness of it. I think it adds a new dimension to me."

"And what dimension might that be?" Marion asked.

"Smoothness. Roundness. Nothing hidden." She liked hearing herself say such things.

"Is this a possible dimension for you?" Marion was curious if anything had changed for the young woman.

"You know, I don't know. I like to think it is. But I know myself. I know nothing has ever been that easy." Charlotte folded her hands in her lap.

"But I feel better since I did it. I feel . . ." She paused. "I don't know, clearheaded, or something." Then she realized the irony of her description.

Marion was impressed. The difference in her client was small but noticeable.

Charlotte continued. "I don't understand a lot of things. I don't know how to have faith or keep faith or grow faith. I don't think that I'm much of a pastor. I don't know who God is or how God is or sometimes even if God is; and I don't really seem to understand my place in the world."

She reached up and ran her hand across her slick, bald head. "But today," she said with a great deal of confidence, "today I'm okay with not understanding any of those things. Today, all I know is that I got a head that's shaped like a question mark, I'm lucky enough to have some very good people in my life, and I have spent way too much time wrestling with things."

Charlotte took in a breath. "And that's all I know."

She turned to Marion, who was smiling at her. "Does that make sense?"

"Naming what you know is a powerful place to start," the older woman answered. "And that's a powerful place to go back to when you get all tangled up." She paused.

"Naming what you know." The young minister said it like a mantra.

They spent the last forty minutes talking about Charlotte's idea of fun and what she wanted to add to her life. They talked about her father and whether she felt it might be a good time to visit. They talked about Margaret and cancer and the cruel lessons that are learned in illness. And they ended their session the way they had for the previous three appointments, a clasping of both hands as they stood at the door and a reminder from Marion to Charlotte to concentrate on what she had learned and then to let it go.

The young pastor stopped at the garden on her way out and sat down on the bench. The sun warmed her head, and she drew in a long and delightful breath. "I know friendship," she said in a strong and rooted voice, thinking of the women in her church. "I know that." And then she got up and drove to the other side of town.

When she arrived at the doctor's office, the others were already there. They stood in a small circle in the waiting room, their heads small and pale. Charlotte came in and stood near them, feeling their nervousness, their anxiety about what was about to happen.

They took turns holding Margaret's hand; and when Margaret's name was called, much to the surprise of the nurse who had asked for her, all of them proceeded together down the hall, following her through the door of the second room on the right.

Four baldheaded women and one cancer patient crammed themselves into the tiny examination room waiting for the doctor. Margaret had tried to tell them that she didn't need everybody to go with her. But no one wanted her to face the report by herself, and they couldn't decide which ones got to go and which ones had to stay behind and wait.

Louise was the one who said they could all fit in the room but that, even if they couldn't, she was not giving up her space of being with Margaret. "After all," she had said, "I didn't shave my head for nothing. I expect to hear what that doctor's got to say."

Margaret had then agreed that they could all come but that no one was allowed to speak a word, ask any questions, or cry until she had said it was all right. They had all agreed to be quiet.

When Dr. Morgan walked in, it startled him to see so many people in the little room. For a second he stood in the doorway, acting as if he wasn't sure what to do. It was, for him, quite a shock to see four women, heads uncovered and shorn, so blatantly hairless. He had several cancer patients under his care, but none of them had he seen in public without a scarf or hat or wig disguising their baldness.

The women had discussed wearing some covering but then had all agreed that they had nothing to hide and that they were, in fact, proud of their choice of solidarity and proud of their naked scalps.

"Well," Dr. Morgan said as he finally walked in and closed the door behind him, "you all must be the local cancer support group." He knew there was such a group that met; he had just never encountered them.

"I suppose you can call us that," Jessie responded, answering for her friends.

"Well, Margaret, it is important to surround yourself with positive energy. Cancer survivors need to hear from one another in order to stay healthy and positive."

He smiled at the women, then sat down on the stool in front of Margaret. He opened her chart and began to read silently.

Beatrice thought maybe they should tell the doctor that they weren't cancer patients, just sympathetic friends. But she remembered her promise to be quiet and decided to let him think what he wanted to think.

The four women stood behind Margaret as she sat on the examining table. She had already had her tube removed, already been through one follow-up visit. This was the appointment at which she would hear the surgery pathology report and the recommendations of the doctors on her team for further treatment.

Margaret took in a deep breath, trying to be calm. She had tried to prepare herself for anything, radiation, chemotherapy, more surgery. She was trying to remain open and positive. She felt the closeness of her friends and was glad they were with her.

Charlotte reached up and placed her hand on Margaret's shoulder.

"Well, this is a great report." Dr. Morgan kept studying it; then he put the folder down and focused on his patient. "I have talked to Dr. Miller; and as your oncologist and general physician, we both agree that with the radiologist's findings, that at least for now, you don't need any further treatment."

Charlotte patted Margaret's shoulder, letting out a huge sigh.

"There were seventeen lymph nodes taken and not one of them was cancerous. The tumor was small and contained, and I just don't think we should do anything else at the present time."

"Thank you, Jesus," Jessie whispered and clapped her hands.

"Some patients choose to do a few rounds of chemo for a little extra insurance, but at this point, I think it would just be a waste." He peered back down at the papers in his lap. "We'll follow you closely for the next year to make sure."

Margaret took him by the hand. "Thank you so much."

"You're welcome."

He turned to the other women. "So, I guess you'll have one group member who won't have the same haircut."

Then he smiled. "I'll see you in a month and Dr. Miller wants to see you in a couple of weeks. You had your follow-up visit, right?"

Margaret nodded.

"Everything all right with that?"

She nodded again. "He says it's healing up nicely."

"Good," he replied. "Well then, is there anything else you need?"

Margaret shook her head.

"Okay." He stood up from his seat. "Nice to meet all of you." And with that, he turned and walked out the door.

The room exploded into screams and laughter. They hugged each other, and all of them fell on top of Margaret and into a great mass of joyful women. It was the miracle they had all prayed for but were afraid to mention. It was the very best report they could have heard. And they pulled together and then apart and jumped and danced about, all in a fit of sheer pleasure.

The women were so completely overjoyed that it took a while before anyone thought of anything other than the perfect news. They luxuriated in the word, relishing the moment. Finally, after a few minutes, Louise understood what else this visit meant. Margaret wasn't going to lose her hair. She froze in the thought while the others continued to celebrate.

"Beatrice Newgarden Witherspoon!" she suddenly yelled. "I cannot believe that you talked us into shaving our heads! I cannot believe that I let you talk *me* into shaving *my* head!" Then she reached over, trying to grab Beatrice.

"Somebody better call that doctor back in here because I figure I'm about to strangle you!" And she knocked over the stool and the trash can trying to get to Beatrice.

Beatrice jumped out of the way to the other side of the table, next to the sink. "Somebody help me!" she cried out.

"Wait! Wait!" It was Margaret. She was trying to get in between them without getting too close since she was still sore. "Louise, leave Beatrice alone! She was only trying to help!"

Louise kept straining to grab the other woman, lunging across the table, reaching around Margaret, while Jessie and Charlotte moved out of the way, laughing.

"That's the whole problem! She's always trying to help!" She yanked and pulled at the air. "And now I'm baldheaded 'cause she's always trying to help."

Jessie shouted, "Oh, Lou, stop, just be glad she only wanted to shave our heads!"

Beatrice scrambled to get away from Louise by dodging her snatching, grabbing fingers and trying to stay behind Margaret. There was a lot of noise, and finally a nurse had to come into the room and ask them all to leave.

Beatrice ran out first, followed closely by Louise. Jessie was behind, trying to restrain them both, while Charlotte and Margaret remained in the room.

"What about you?" Margaret asked her preacher. "You mind being bald?"

Charlotte shook her head and noted herself in the mirror that was on the wall near the door. "Nah, I sort of like it. Makes me look kind of like a monk or something.

"What about you?" she asked Margaret. "You think you might shave just because you feel sorry for us, so you can be one with the rest of us?"

The older woman turned to the preacher. "Not unless somebody's ready to give up a breast and be one with me. I don't think so!"

They walked out together and joined the other women in the parking lot. Louise and Beatrice were out of breath from chasing each other. Jessie was standing at the driver's side with the door open.

"Well, what shall we do after hearing this great news?" Jessie was the one to ask.

"I think an ice cream sundae is the perfect treat," Margaret replied.

"I know just the spot," Jessie said as she got into the car, "a great place to go after mammograms and doctor visits."

Margaret smiled. "Or just to honor life," she added, remembering the last time she had gone to the restaurant with her friend, the light and hopeful conversation they had shared, the cool surprise of ice cream on her tongue.

Jessie stuck her arm out the window, raising her hand in the air, while the other women climbed in the back of the car. Charlotte took the middle seat to keep Louise and Beatrice, who were still bickering, separated. Margaret sat in the front.

And the women drove out of the parking lot and out past a hill of gardens. And the earth, teeming with silent seeds and full-fisted bulbs, crept outside itself to witness the noisy celebration of women well on their way, sowing life.

THE GARDENER'S PRAYER

I drop a seed into the earth
I dare not think it's mine
I cover it. I water it.
I pray the sun will shine.

I build a fence around it
To guard from wandering feet
I cushion it with straw and hay,
Protecting it from heat.

And every day I stand and ask
Will heaven see my gift?
Is it deep enough and warm enough?
Will God pass by and lift

The life that rests within that seed?
The faith desired to grow?
I wait. I pray. I hope. I cheer.
And one day soon, I'll know.

❋

Welcome Back to Hope Springs!

Now that you've met Beatrice, Charlotte, Louise, Jessie, and Margaret, you can get to know them better through the Hope Springs trilogy. *Friendship Cake*, the bestselling first book in the series, and *Forever Friends*, the third installment, are available at your local bookstore now.

For ideas for your own book club, as well as tidbits and advice from the ladies of Hope Springs and from Lynne Hinton herself, please make sure to visit www.LynneHinton.com.

Hope Springs Reader's Guide

QUESTIONS FOR DISCUSSION

1. Lynne Hinton has stated that her grandmother, to whom the book and the opening poem are dedicated, taught her to garden. Is there anyone in your life who taught you to love the earth? What does gardening mean to you?

2. Charlotte realizes that she doesn't have anything to offer her suicidal parishioner, Nadine. What do you consider an appropriate pastoral response to a person who attempted suicide?

3. The doctor is concerned about his patient Margaret when they discuss the findings from her mammogram. He wonders "what kind of support systems she had, what gave her purpose, and how well she could fight trouble." What are the resources you think a person needs when facing an illness?

4. Charlotte decides to see a therapist. What are your thoughts about a minister going into counseling?

5. Jessie discusses her desire to move from Hope Springs, her hometown. Have you ever desired to live in a place other than where you live? Where would you choose to move and why?

6. Marion, Charlotte's therapist, asks the young pastor to tell how she thinks of God. How do you think of God? How comfortable are you with a feminine image of God?

7. Margaret, Louise, and Beatrice discuss what makes a woman, a woman. What are your thoughts about what distinguishes a woman from a man? Is it physical or emotional?

8. In order for Nadine to begin to heal regarding her loss she must forgive herself for what she considered her responsibility in the accident that killed her daughter. How does a person learn to forgive themself? What helps in encouraging the forgiveness of oneself?

9. Jessie realizes her fears that James will leave her again. Are you surprised that she took him back when she did? How does a couple who has separated and come back together regain the trust that was lost?

10. Why do you think the women decided to shave their heads? What displays of empathy and friendship have you experienced in your life? How important is friendship in facing illness?

11. Jessie and James decide to take a trip to Africa. What trip have you always wanted to take? Where would you go if you could go anywhere?

12. Nadine decides that she wants to keep the spirit of Brittany alive by continuing to be involved in the things the little girl

enjoyed, to love as she had loved. What ways have you heard that people keep the spirit alive of those who have died?

13. How is gardening a metaphor for life and death?

14. How do Bea's Botanical Bits address life? Are any relevant to your life?

15. After shaving her head, Jessie remembers her mother's insistence on having neat hair. In her conversation with James, she remembers her childhood trauma of straightening and washing and caring for her hair. Did you ever have fights with your mother about your hair? Why are hairstyles and length of hair such issues for women?

16. During Charlotte's last session with Marion she was supposed to discuss plans she had made to bring fun into her life. What "fun" would you add into your life if this was your assignment?

17. Charlotte confesses during a session to Marion that she doesn't know a lot about faith; but that for that day, at least, she was comfortable in the unknowing. How much of faith is the acceptance of not understanding God?

18. Marion confirms that naming what you do know is a powerful tool for the spiritual journey. Charlotte knows friendship. What do you know?

19. In the end, the act of shaving their heads becomes a significant personal event for a few of the women. What do you think this act meant for each of them?

20. After the good news from the doctor, the women go out to eat ice cream. Where do you go to celebrate? What's your celebration food?

Forever Friends

THE WOMEN OF HOPE SPRINGS COMMUNITY CHURCH HAVE weathered some pretty fierce storms: Louise's unrequited love for her best friend, Charlotte's struggle to find her own place in the community, and Jessie's yearning for a life outside of the small Southern town. Now, the bonds of friendship are tested again when Margaret learns whether or not she is cancer free, and Beatrice learns some surprising secrets about life in Hope Springs—and about the value of trust in any relationship. But what do the friends do when they discover that one of their own is leaving? Join Louise, Jessie, Charlotte, Beatrice, and Margaret for an homage to friendship you'll never forget.

❋

FROM CHAPTER 1

Be careful of that desk drawer."

The warning came too late. Charlotte walked right around the corner and into the open bottom drawer and nicked her shin, ripping a large hole in her hose and causing a painful contusion just below her knee.

"Gosh. Sorry about that." The desk sergeant winced at the sight of the young woman's leg. "That desk needs to be put somewhere else." She made a clucking noise with her tongue on the roof of her mouth. "You're the second one to run into it this morning."

Charlotte started to ask why the woman hadn't moved the desk aside herself or, at the very least, taped the gaping drawer shut, but since she was not one to make such bold suggestions, especially to strangers who wore guns and handcuffs on their belts, she simply bent down and calculated the damage.

There was a little blood from the gash, but the worst consequence was the unsightly rip she now had in her stockings. She knew there wasn't any way to hide the tear, and she wished she had followed her instincts when she was getting ready and wore pants instead of this dress and panty hose or, even better, that she had listened to her original inclination, which was not to come in the first place.

She was at the correctional facility in Winston-Salem to visit Peggy DuVaughn's grandson, Lamont, who was in jail on a robbery charge. Peggy asked Charlotte to go because she was concerned about his safety and well-being and because she had heard that ministers had unlimited opportunities to see inmates, whereas family members had strict rules about their visitations.

"It's different this time," the older woman said to her pastor after she finally confessed what it was that was troubling her. "He's really going to do better. I know it."

Charlotte had assumed when her parishioner called and asked if she could drop by and talk that she was concerned about her husband, Vastine. His doctor had given him a terminal diagnosis of congestive heart failure and he had only recently become a hospice patient. But the older woman had come into the office and fidgeted and changed the subject from first one thing and then another until Charlotte finally asked what she was doing there. Peggy broke down and told her about her youngest daughter's son, who had gotten mixed up with the wrong crowd in junior high school and had never gotten away from it.

"It's those drugs," she said as if she knew for sure the cause of his downfall. "They get hooked on that stuff and then there's just no way to save them." She tugged at the back of her collar and dropped her hands in her lap. "It's the devil's work," she added with a pained expression.

Charlotte nodded in sympathy with a passing thought of Serena, remembering her own hopes for a family member's recovery.

"Vastine and I tried to keep him, you know, when he was little. Sherry was going through the divorce then and just had so much on her." The older woman's face was pinched and crossed in worry. "We kept him for almost three years."

Charlotte had not heard this part of the DuVaughn family history.

"He was such a sweet boy." Peggy rubbed her hands together. "He and Vastine were real close." Then she paused, looking up. "We never had boys."

Charlotte listened. She knew there were three daughters, Sherry, Bernice, and Madison. They had all attended the church at one time or another. Madison's oldest child had been confirmed at Hope Springs. Charlotte thought she was at college out of state somewhere.

"Little Lamont was a handful, but we were doing the best we could." She stopped. "We got him enrolled in the kindergarten at the school. We put him in Scouts and baseball."

She sat quietly for a few moments.

"We would have kept him, you know." Then she sighed with the sound of regret. "But he got to be too much for us." Peggy shifted from side to side in her chair. "So Sherry took him back and they moved down to Lexington." Her movement in the chair stopped. "And then things just got worse."

The pastor handed Peggy a tissue. She took it and wiped her eyes.

"It's always been little things before now, mostly just boy stuff. I mean, I knew he was heading in the wrong direction, but I kept thinking he'd grow out of it, mature." She paused. "It was stealing this time," she confessed. "He broke into a convenience store. Tried to get into the cash drawer but was only able to take some merchandise. When they caught him," she hesitated and shook her head, "he had a gun."

The older woman wiped her eyes again. "It's serious." She peered up at Charlotte. "He's in the adult unit. They say he threatened the police officer." She dropped her head. "He's definitely going to prison. I saw him when he first got there. He was so scared he cried." Peggy spoke softly. "It just about broke my heart."

Charlotte went around her desk and knelt down in front of her parishioner.

"Sherry won't have anything to do with him, says she's through, told me not to waste my time trying to help him."

The pastor reached up and placed her hand on Peggy's shoulder.

"But how can a mother, a grandmother, let one of her babies stay in a place like that and not visit, not try to get him out? He was so scared," she said again as she reached in her purse for another tissue and held it in her hands.

Charlotte nodded, a gesture of sympathy, but she still did not speak.

The older woman looked down at the young minister kneeling in front of her. "I can only visit on Friday nights, for just fifteen minutes," she said, leading up to the request. "But I was thinking that maybe you could go, say you're his pastor." Peggy hesitated. "Maybe you can check on him today or tomorrow." She seemed embarrassed. "If you could just go and make sure he's okay."

Charlotte wasn't sure what to say. She had never gone to a jail before, and the sudden request from her church member was disconcerting.

"Peggy," the minister replied sincerely, "I'm not sure they'll let me see him."

The older woman nodded submissively. "I understand. You don't even know him. And it is a big thing to ask of you to go all the way over there."

Charlotte rolled back to rest on her heels and read the woman's face. Peggy DuVaughn was quiet but strong. She wasn't really a leader in the church, not very active or outspoken, but watching her as she sat in the pastor's office, so broken and vulnerable, Charlotte thought of who she had been in the church, of all of the years that Peggy had been caring for her husband, years without complaint or request, years of displayed gratitude for her church's support and her pastor's visits.

Peggy always thanked Charlotte for her prayers, even wrote her notes from time to time to tell her how much the sermons on tape had meant to the two of them when they were unable to attend the worship services, how appreciative

they both were for her care during her husband's more criti-
cal times.

Charlotte focused on the older woman, thinking that she had
believed that Peggy's only problem had been Vastine's health,
that this was all she thought about or dealt with or worried over.
The pastor felt surprised and sad to learn that Peggy had been
troubled for so long about her grandson and that she had never
felt free enough to say anything to her pastor or to anyone else
in the church.

The burden of shame for this woman, she thought to herself,
is as serious as Vastine's heart condition. This disappointment
and regret, this dysfunction of her family, has broken her and
chained her spirit even more than her husband's terminal illness. Peggy DuVaughn had borne the weight of her grandson's
addiction and troubles in silence, as if his choices, his mistakes,
were a reflection of her years of care or lack of care, depending
on which situation she felt more guilty about.

"Of course I'll try," Charlotte said to Peggy. "I'll call the
chaplain this afternoon and see if they'll let me see him."

And that had been it. With that promise made to her
parishioner less than twenty-four hours earlier, she had visited
Margaret to tell her that she was not able to go with her and
the other friends to her doctor's appointment, and she was
now standing in the Forsyth County Jail, her panty hose
ruined, her leg cut and bleeding, and she was about to go
behind guarded and locked doors to visit an armed thief she
had never laid eyes on.

"You'll need to leave your purse in one of those."

The desk sergeant pointed to the lockers on the wall to their
right. "It's fifty cents," she added.

Charlotte pulled out her wallet and took out two quarters. She walked over and placed the change in the slots and opened the locker. She put her purse inside, remembering that she had already given her driver's license to another police officer and hoping that she wouldn't forget it. She shut the door and pulled out the key. She walked back to the sergeant.

"Okay, just stand there and they'll open that door for you. Then you'll be in a waiting cell and they'll open the next set of doors. Then you turn to the left, and the visiting booths will be right in front of you. A guard will send the prisoner to you in a few minutes. Just wait until he comes."

Then the sergeant left Charlotte standing in front of a large steel door before the minister was able to ask the woman to repeat the instructions.

Suddenly, the large door in front of her opened, and she heard a voice on the intercom telling her to step inside. When she did, the door shut hard behind her. A few seconds passed, and another door in front slid open with a loud clang. She stepped through the doorway and it closed. She scanned the area to her right and then to her left, noticing a hallway with a set of doors. She moved in that direction, aware that she was being watched, and opened one of the doors in front of her. It was a small chamber with a stool in front of a large glass window, a telephone receiver hanging on the right.

She walked in as the door shut behind her and sat down on the stool, wondering if someone was still observing her.

Through the window before her, Charlotte was able to see to the other side, where there was a narrow hallway. Several inmates walked past in bright orange coveralls. A couple of them stared at her as they passed by. She tried to appear unalarmed and unafraid as she sat waiting for her visit to begin. There were sounds of men laughing and doors opening and closing; it seemed that at least fifteen minutes had passed since she had been inside the booth.

She was just about to go out and ask for assistance when, finally, she heard a door on the other side of the booth open. Two men, one a guard, the other an inmate, walked by her, passing without any attention, and then turned around and walked back. They stood directly in front of her.

"Lamont?" she asked but wasn't sure they could hear her. Then the young man in the orange suit nodded.

Follow Charlotte's journey with Beatrice, Louise, Jessie, and Margaret in *Forever Friends* available now from HarperSanFrancisco.

Come Back to Hope Springs!